BORN BROKEN

BORN BROKEN

The Mistakes That Medicine Made

T.J. WILTSHIRE

authorHOUSE®

AuthorHouse™ UK Ltd.
1663 Liberty Drive *
Bloomington, IN 47403 USA
www.authorhouse.co.uk
Phone: 0800.197.4150

Published by AuthorHouse   02/15/2014

ISBN: 978-1-4918-9005-9 (sc)
ISBN: 978-1-4918-9423-1 (e)

Library of Congress Control Number: 2014902634

CONTENTS

For Everyone

1940s

AND THE CREST OF SUBMISSION

3290 DAYS. 3150 tiles on the ceiling of the dormitory, 5488 in the day room. Fourteen patients on the ward—Ward 51—including myself. My parents admitted me here because I do not talk. My captors think that means I am retarded; they all talk around me like I cannot hear them. I let them continue to think that, mostly because telling them would require talking, but also because being quiet benefits me here. I am seen as "less difficult". I am treated with more leniency than the fat woman who thinks she is the Virgin Mary, or the old woman who shouts to the air. I live under a disguise of incompetence, yet I am intelligent enough to have figured out that the ward is supplied with its drugs every other Friday; the captors are more hesitant to stab at us when they are low on drugs.

At 7:00 am, the grey dress with the white apron comes in to dress and wash me. Today, it is the nice nurse; she lets me dress myself once I shrug her away. I do not like people touching me.

I am given the derivative task of sweeping, which I do invisibly. No one notices the mute with the broom. I sometimes clean the captors' offices. I am good at sweeping. It takes me exactly 467 strokes; my personal best is 8 minutes 5 seconds. Under constant supervision. It drives the paranoid woman insane. She is normally dragged kicking and screaming to the padded room, and when she comes back she will be calmer for a day or two with new puncture wounds on her arms. The ones we all have: our crest of submission. The drugs we are given when we are "difficult" make your head foggy. You are disorientated for a few days. I do not like it.

At 10:34pm, I creep out of bed so as not to wake the other women; I pick the lock with two hairpins I had lifted from a bad nurse, and slip out of the dormitory. I take my regular walk around the corridors, avoiding Night Nurse's patrol route (which I had spent my first 4 nights here studying). I hear a noise I have not encountered before. It is a strange noise, almost a shuffling sound. I cling to the wall and peer around the corner: There is a captor with his back to me, trousers low enough for me to see his buttocks, and a nurse—the nice nurse from this morning—with her grey dress ruffled up around her waist. The captor pushes her against the wall. The nice nurse cries, but does not make a sound because the captor has one hand firmly clasped over her mouth; though he is the one making the peculiar noise. I do not like people crying. My mother tried to teach me how to comfort a crying person. I was not very good at it. The captor lets out a louder noise; it almost sounds like he is stifling a cry himself. I try to remember where I have heard a similar noise before . . . When the memory comes to me, I recoil and feel my cheeks go warm. The captor and nurse are doing sex. I remember the noise from when the woman from bed 12 had told everyone about her honeymoon. Noises and actions included. She had been taken to the padded room.

I peer around the corner again, out of necessity, since they are blocking my route. The captor has gone, but the nurse sits on the floor, sobbing into her palms. Then, remembering my manners and my mother's voice, I stealthily make my way across the thirty feet gap between us and sit down next to the nice nurse. She flinches when I tap her shoulder, and chokes as she looks up and sees me.

'Oh . . . you shouldn't be out of bed, Andrea,' she stammers.

I shrug. Nice Nurse sighs.

'I'm a right old mess . . . I don't know what I'm going to do . . . Oh God . . .'

I am not sure if she is talking to herself or me. It is an awkward nine-second silence. Almost silence, Nice Nurse is still sobbing.

'. . . Did he not say please?' I murmur. Talking for the first time in 11 years and 7 days; my voice sounds raspy.

Nice Nurse gasps at the sound of my vocal chords working. She looks at me wide eyed.

'Did he not say please?' I repeat. Mother taught me to say "please" when I want something.

The repetition shakes Nice Nurse out of her shock. 'No . . . no he didn't. The bastard should die . . .'

Andrea Garcia underwent a lobotomy on the 11th February 1942. She was the seventh person out of fifteen in the UK to receive this operation after a mental breakdown during which she stabbed a well-respected doctor through the chest with a fountain pen while sweeping his office. The cause of her actions is unknown, and she was incapable of explaining herself. As a result, Miss Garcia is now in a vegetative state.

AND THE TAPS LEFT RUNNING

ALICE HAS ALWAYS been odd. Mother had told me on several occasions that when she was a baby, she didn't smile or make cute baby noises—though she hadn't really acknowledged this until she had taken Alice to one of Joyce's famous get-togethers. Alice had been the only baby not screaming, crying or laughing. Mother told me that Albert—Evelyn's husband—had made a remark in his deep, booming voice that Alice was "broken". A few people had chuckled mockingly, clearly having noticed my sister's vacant expression. Mother had been horrified and embarrassed, so we had left soon afterwards. My parents were very concerned about social and public appearances, the degree to which you'll soon understand.

When Alice hadn't started talking by the age of five, my parents were thrown into a fit of despair. They immediately presumed she was retarded, you see. They called various experts and had her tested, during which it was found that she excelled in the intelligence tests, so they all concluded that she would start talking when she was ready. What my parents hadn't realized was that from about the age of four, Alice spoke to me. I don't mean to say she spoke every time they left the room, but whenever she had something she needed to say, it was to me.

However I had no intention of sharing this information with our parents; not just because of the pride I felt being her confidant, but also because I knew that if they'd found out, they would think that she wasn't talking to spite them. This would bring on more punishment than she was already given.

My parents were very embarrassed about Alice's "condition", as they called it, and on the rare occasions we had guests over, she would be sent to her room. I think Alice preferred being alone in her room as opposed to being downstairs with the half-hearted discussions about school, hobbies, and how it was "just wonderful that the war was over", which I had to politely sit through.

I'd have been eighteen at the time of this next anecdote; at Oxford studying Social and Preventative Medicine—a fact my parents boasted about to anyone who would listen. Alice was being tutored at home to reduce the attention she might draw (and the embarrassment she might cause) in school. I had come home for the weekend, at my father's request, since a friend of his, Doctor Browne, was apparently a good connection to have. On this occasion, Dr. Browne had inquired as to Alice's whereabouts when we retired to the lounge for drinks. My father, who hadn't had to make an excuse for a while, had ducked his head to hide the perspiration and mumbled that she wasn't feeling well and so she was in her room. He then subtly dabbed his brow with his handkerchief while Dr. Browne started glancing around the room, interested in the art my parents had collected.

Alice was thirteen and still didn't speak in front of our parents; she'd often fail to acknowledge them if they tried to talk to her. It drove them insane, but I found it amusing and admirable that she disregarded them and their authority so openly and in a way that I thought I never could. Until now.

I frowned at my father as he reeled off some symptoms associated with a mild stomach ache and interrupted Dr. Browne in expressing his concern.

'When I went to greet her not an hour ago she seemed in perfect health.' I tried not to make it obvious that I was shaking.

My father scowled, and in that moment I could see my status as "golden child" had been shattered by my supposed betrayal. Dr. Browne glanced between the two of us, clearly confused by my father's sudden animosity towards me. He placed his scotch glass onto the coffee table and heaved himself out of the armchair that had taken his fancy.

'I could go up and have a look at her for you, Bernard,' he offered, I assume in an attempt to diffuse the situation. 'Just to make sure she *is* okay.' He looked at me as he added to his proposal, no doubt thinking I had been attempting to undermine my father.

'No, no, Rodney, it's quite alright,' my father hurriedly replied, his round face turning a deep crimson.

'Are you sure? I might be able to prescribe something for her,' Dr. Browne continued.

'No!' My father raised his voice, and Dr. Browne looked shocked for a whole five-or-so seconds before regaining his composure.

My mother, however, found it much more difficult to remain calm. Her knees buckled in the doorway and she fell, dropping the tray of glasses she had collected. They shattered upon impact with the floor, and I moved towards her to check for injury.

'Leave her, Leonard. Go to your room', my father snapped, seething. 'Now!'

I stopped mid-step towards my clearly unconscious mother and cleared my throat, attempting to bite back all the resentful comments that had gathered over the years.

'Fine,' I eventually grunted. 'It was a pleasure to meet you, Dr. Browne.' I still had manners. My grudge wasn't with him. Yet.

I trudged up the stairs, listening to Dr. Browne giving instructions to my father to aid him in bringing my mother back to consciousness. Alice was giggling in her room, so I knocked at her door. It swung open as soon as my knuckles moved back to my side, so she had most likely heard me coming up the stairs.

'Leo!' It was more of a label than a greeting, and she had already turned, heading back to her pile of books.

I could still hear the conversation downstairs, thanks to Dr. Browne's naturally loud voice, so I tried to tune them out a little.

'I thought I would come and check you hadn't turned on all the taps and left them running again,' I chuckled, remembering several occasions where the bathroom was flooded as a result of Alice's love of water.

'If I had, it would have eventually come through the ceiling again, so you could have easily deduced that I have not turned on any taps before even coming upstairs,' she deadpanned.

'You caught me, I just wanted to come and see my favourite sister.' I grinned as she glanced at me.

'I'm your only sister, Leonard.'

'Love you too.' I rolled my eyes. 'Anyway, what book are you reading?' I was genuinely curious, as she tended to read at a much more advanced level than her age dictated. She merely gestured to the array of open books, all at various stages of completion on her floor.

'May I have a look?' I had learnt not to touch anything of Alice's without having asked first. She nodded her approval, too engrossed in a particularly large book to pay me much attention. I picked up the closest book to me and sat cross-legged on the floor opposite her. 'The Pearl, by John Steinbeck—not bad.'

'It's about a Mexican fisherman.'

'I know, I read it not too long ago.'

'Were you older than me when you read it?' she asked, looking up at me from the book in her hands.

'Yes, I think it was just last year.'

A small smile played on her lips. 'So you were seventeen?'

'Yes,' I resigned.

Alice's smile grew; she always treasured the knowledge that she was of a more advanced intellect than most people—though she would argue *all* people.

We quickly fell back into silence, as was usually the case. I scanned the room briefly, noticing the regimented order of the bookcase that hadn't changed from when we were younger and I had read to Alice. The old dolls—that she had never played with in the traditional sense—were lined up along the windowsill, in height order.

'. . . sending my daughter to one of *those* places, Rodney,' my father bellowed below us.

My ears pricked up, and suddenly all my attention was focused on the two men downstairs.

'Trust me, Bernard, it's the best thing for her. It's admirable that you've put up with her for so long, but she obviously causes you and Florence a lot of stress.' Dr. Browne sounded sympathetic, but also condescending.

So, my father had told him about Alice—this much I had figured out, but I was at a loss as to where they were discussing sending her. *One of those places* obviously held stigma from the strained tone my father used. The thought of Alice being sent *anywhere* made my stomach clench. I glanced at her, worried she might have overheard as well, but she was still engrossed in her book. I excused myself and retired to my room to think.

When I woke the next morning, I was confused. I glanced at the clock; 7:30am, much earlier than my body clock usually woke me. Then my brain caught up with my ears and registered the screaming.

I shot up from my bed and out of my bedroom like a drunken fool in yesterday's clothes. Then I scrambled down the stairs, slipping down the last few and landing painfully on the small of my back. An immense shooting pain ripped through my spine. With tears stinging my eyes, I hauled myself up and followed the screaming to the front of the house. I threw the front door open and half ran, half limped to the car. I stopped at the back window. Alice was on the back seat, her knees tucked up under her chin, screaming. Her eyes were glassy as she glanced at me, and I briefly placed my hand on the glass of the window before looking across to our parents. My father was talking to my mother, and I could see the exasperation on his face. Mother was crying.

'You've broken her routine, that's why she won't stop screaming, Bernard,' she was explaining through her tears.

'What the bloody hell is going on?' I shouted as I edged my way closer to them. The pain in my back was making me angrier, and the crippling fear wasn't doing me any favours in my attempt to remain calm.

'Your sister is going to Greymore.' My father barely glanced at me as he spat the words out.

'What is—you're sending her to an *asylum*?' I yelled.

Greymore Mental Institution was a few miles away; some friends and I used to cycle down there in attempt to see some of the crazy people when we were younger.

'Dr. Browne said she's probably schizophrenic,' Father stated, nonchalant.

'Dr. Browne isn't a psychiatric doctor! He's a bloody General Practitioner! You're sending your daughter into a hell hole because of what some stupid-'

My father spun round to face me. 'Don't you dare question my decision. It's your fault for bringing Alice to his attention last night in your ridiculous attempt to undermine me!' He pointed his fat finger at me.

'So it wasn't your decision at all, it was Dr. Browne's-'

'He merely pointed me in the right direction, and gave me the advice I've needed to hear for a good few years!'

'No!' I screamed. 'No, you're just conforming to what people in a position of authority tell you to do. You always have. Heaven forbid you do something without the approval of society!'

My body was shaking, and my back was in agonising pain. I'd barely inhaled before I saw my father's fist swinging towards me. All the anger, shock, guilt and pain stopped me from reacting in any way other than just letting the punch connect. My head snapped back, and I heard my nose crunch. It's embarrassing, but I crumpled to the floor. I heard my mother gasp, but she did not move.

'I'll fix this, Alice, I swear to God!' I managed to shout, one hand digging into the dusty grit of the driveway, the other outstretched towards the car that was now leaving with my baby sister inside.

She isn't insane, was my last thought before the gravel, my mother's ankles, and the road Alice was now disappearing down went black.

*   *   *

Alice was a very eccentric looking thirteen year old. She had dark red hair, similar to the colour of copper, which fell in loose ringlets to her shoulders. Her dark blue eyes contrasted her clear porcelain skin, which had light freckles dotted across the bridge of her nose and cheekbones. She was an early bloomer, and while her breasts had not developed to a huge size, they were noticeable, even under the huge grey shirt that threatened to engulf her.

Upon her arrival, her belt and shoelaces had been confiscated as part of standard procedure. Her screaming had stopped when the car had turned into the gates of the institution and she had realized she was being locked away. She remembered seeing her brother running towards the car, pausing, and then continuing towards their parents. Father had hit Leonard. She could also recall hearing Leonard shout as their father had driven away. He had shouted her name. The sound of his voice flooded her memory: *'I'll fix this, Alice, I swear to God!'*

She smiled. Leonard would come and get her from this place, and she would be able to return to her room and her books. This thought is what allowed her to be nudged by her father towards the waiting nurse. This thought is what allowed her to be led through the institution's women's ward and to her allocated bed. There was a pile of grey round-neck t-shirts, vests, button up trousers and slip on shoes on top of the sheets.

'Your father must have friends in high places for you to have been given shoes; make sure you keep a tight grip on them,' the nurse was saying.

Alice did not say anything to the nurse, but nodded to show her understanding, hoping this would inspire the old lady to leave.

She didn't.

'You are to be awake, washed and dressed by 8:30am; your ward's wash time is 8:05am—you will have 10 minutes. Lights go out at 9:00pm. There are no exceptions, you are to abide by Greymore's rules.'

Alice decided she no longer liked this nurse, who had been polite and had even smiled in front of her father.

'You are required to change into standard Greymore patient attire immediately.'

Alice stared, waiting for the nurse to leave, but no such move was made.

The nurse glared. 'You do not want to become a difficult patient.'

Alice inhaled deeply, turning her back to the nurse as she started removing her shirt. Her skin itched as a second pair of hands joined her own. The nurse took the shirt off Alice's shoulders, pulling it down her arms and proceeded to unhook her bra.

'These are confiscated for safety purposes,' she explained as Alice shrugged the bra off. Alice felt invaded; the nurse was being more intrusive than necessary. She screamed then, the discomfort building to a point that she could no longer handle. The nurse didn't bat an eye as she called the two young men who had moved to stand in the hallway when the patient's back had turned. Alice didn't see the needle, so when she was sedated for the first time it came as a shock, and caught her off guard. She crumpled into the young men's arms; topless and vulnerable.

'What do you mean I can't see her? She's my sister!' The young man raised his voice, his face almost turning as red as his hair.

'I'm sorry, dear, but it says right here in her documents that the only people authorised to visit her are her parents.' The woman on the other end of the phone was trying her best to sound sympathetic, but doing a bad job; she could not understand why anyone would want to visit the nutters that had been sectioned at Greymore.

The young man clutched at his hair, grunted a sarcastic thank you, then slammed down the phone and stormed out of the phone box.

When Alice woke up, she was laid down awkwardly and her head felt fuzzy, a sharp pain seared across her temples. When she tried opening her eyes, they met a harsh light, so she scrunched them closed again. Deliberating for a moment, she turned her head to the side and tried a second time, avoiding the glare of the light. She was in a different room, made obvious by the padded walls and the range of stains that had been there for various lengths of time: some were years old, others only a few days.

As she tried to sit up she was met with restraint. She strained to lift her head and looked down at her body, which was strapped to a poor excuse for a bed—more a table. The leather straps were tight and cut into her skin. She still had nothing covering her chest. She struggled against the straps for a moment, but to no avail. A door opened that Alice hadn't noticed because it was covered in the same padding as the walls. A short fat man with a mass of black frizzy hair entered the room and sat on a simple chair that he had carried in with him. He had an air of overconfidence about him that would be enough for anyone to take an instant dislike to him. Alice didn't like him because he had a ridiculous beard with the same frizz consistency as his hair. Alice added a developing bruise around his right eye to her list of characteristics about the man. She frowned, feeling uneasy.

'Miss Yoder, I'm so glad to see you're awake again.' The man grinned, showing far too much teeth.

Again? Alice's brow furrowed with confusion.

'You don't remember our little scene yesterday?' His grin widened. 'I'm Doctor Hunter. We met yesterday when I was sent to establish your diagnosis. I observed you for about an hour before you had quite the violent episode.' He gestured to his eye. 'We had to give you quite a high dosage of . . .' He looked down at her for a moment, as if fondly remembering the moment she was sedated. 'I'm talking to you as though you will actually understand.' He chuckled. 'Anyway, you have been officially sectioned as an egomaniacal schizophrenic with mental retardation.'

He paused, watching to see how Alice would react. She gave no facial response, but within the confines of her mind, she was scared: scared of the implications of being diagnosed as mentally insane. Alice was also stunned she had suffered such an intense memory loss; she had never forgotten anything in her life.

'It's lucky, really, that your father finally told someone about you. It's luckier still that he told a doctor who could guide him to the right decision. Now you're at Greymore, you are no longer a threat to society or your family. Lord only knows what chaos you would have caused if you had been allowed around people. You could have inflicted some serious injury; or worse still, killed someone . . .'

Alice spent the rest of the hour fighting back tears as Doctor Hunter tormented her with harsh words. Worse still, in Alice's opinion, was during the long silences when she watched him stare at her still bare chest. When he had commented on her "ridiculously huge breasts" for her age, she had almost flinched. It made her feel dirty. But she refused to give him a visible reaction, and when Dr. Hunter realized he wasn't going to get one, he made to leave the room—the glint in his eye dimmed slightly. On his way out, he called for a nurse to release Miss Yoder and escort her back to her allocated sleeping quarters on Ward 11. Then he was gone down the hallway into the maze that was Greymore Mental Institution, and Alice exhaled heavily.

When Alice's feet touched the floor, her legs wobbled and she had to lean heavily on the nurse who looked less happy than Alice felt, but neither said anything. Where the straps had been, bruises were developing quickly, and there was dry blood where the leather had bit into her skin. As she walked down the cold corridors, she thought about the memory loss she had suffered. It was new to her: forgetting. Alice could remember everything that she had seen and heard from the age of five. She could memorise whole texts, conversations, and events. With people, she remembered their most distinguishing characteristics and their clothing, so she could remember every person she had ever met. So forgetting a whole conversation, event, and a new person unsettled her.

Alice lay in bed among nineteen other women—most of who were in a drug induced sleep, others groaning and fitful. Luckily, Alice had returned too late for her evening medication. She kept her shoes on after returning to her bed—bed four—and finding all of her t-shirts gone, and only the vests remaining. She had not been able to sleep properly for years, and tonight she was glad of that. It was petrifying: a pitch-black room with nineteen strangers, all of whom have been diagnosed as insane. Then again, so had she—in fact, she had been told she was capable of killing someone. The thought brought tears to her eyes. She had been told she was capable of hurting her parents, or Leonard, and this idea saddened her. Alice replayed the day's occurrence with Dr. Hunter, going over everything he had said and how much she had wanted to hit him. She was frustrated that she could not remember giving him the black eye, but at the same time was impressed with herself for inflicting some kind of pain upon him; she smiled at the thought. *Maybe I really am a danger to people . . .* Her hands shook in the darkness and a single tear ran down her cheek.

'Hello?' The voice was soft, but thick with sleep.

'Hello, is this Doctor Reid?'

'It certainly is, to whom am I speaking?'

'My name is Leonard Yoder, I'm a friend of Ben.'

Ben was a young man interning at Greymore, and had been shadowing Dr. Reid for a few months. The two had become quite good friends, in fact.

'I see, and what can I do for you?'

The young man on the other end of the phone inhaled noticeably. 'Don't hang up until I'm finished, ok?'

Dr. Reid hesitated. 'Ok son.'

'My sister has been sectioned at Greymore, I know you work there, and I was hoping you could tell me her diagnosis since no one else will tell me a damn thing. Alice isn't even crazy, I swear. A little eccentric, sure, but she isn't a loon.'

'You know your parents can phone or visit and find out any information you want . . .' Dr. Reid started, but was quickly interrupted by the younger man who was clearly frustrated.

'They refuse to have anything to do with Alice now; they've practically disowned her since dumping her in that place! It's been two weeks and they've not even mentioned her name!' Leonard was irritable; he had hardly slept the last few days. 'I just need to know her diagnosis so I can work on disproving it, please, Dr. Reid, will you help?' Leonard knew he sounded distressed; his voice strained towards the end of his plea as a result of trying not to cry.

Dr. Reid pinched the bridge of his nose. Just telling the lad his sister's diagnosis would cause no harm, and he was clearly desperate for some form of hope.

'I'm not familiar with your sister since I'm usually on the men's ward, but I'll have no trouble finding out for you. Is there a number I can reach you on tomorrow evening?'

'That's bloody fantastic!' Leonard was beaming; his whole mood had so suddenly been lifted, he was a little short of breath. 'Thank you sir, I don't have a telephone, I'm calling from a phone booth, but I'd be honoured to buy you a drink, to show my gratitude.' The boy sounded positively ecstatic, and Dr. Reid was not about to turn down a free drink.

'Sounds good to me, son, there's a pub not far from Greymore . . .'

Alice cracked open an eye and looked around, still wary of straps, padding and Dr. Hunter. Instead she was met with the smiling face of a blond, wavy haired man, no older then thirty-five, who had crow's feet around his brown eyes. Alice scrambled to pull the sheet to her chest, cautious of his doctor's uniform.

'Good morning, Miss Yoder.' The man was still smiling, and held out his hand for her to shake.

Alice stared at the hand until he withdrew it.

'I'm Doctor Reid. Your brother, Leonard, phoned me a few days ago.' He had decided to be blunt, hoping that mentioning the young girl's brother would instill some trust. After seeing in Miss Yoder's file that she had had the pleasure of Dr. Hunter's company not long after she arrived, the young doctor had concluded that the poor girl's tolerance for doctors would not exactly be sky high.

'Your brother believes you have been wrongly sectioned. I've looked through your record and I disagree with Dr. Hunter's diagnosis.' He did not miss the small flinch Alice could not control at the mention of his colleague. 'Or rather, I disagree that he could have arrived at such a specific conclusion so quickly. I have arranged for an observation session tomorrow afternoon.' His smile remained even though Alice did not react. He had not expected immediate progress—Leonard had told him how difficult his sister could be and it lent credence to his suspicions.

Dr. Reid had told Leonard his sister's diagnosis over drinks, and the young man had been furious and frustrated; positive his sister was not retarded or schizophrenic. Dr. Reid had taken it upon himself—especially when he had seen that Dr. Hunter had been the diagnosing doctor— to see if a change in diagnosis could be found, or even a removal of the stamp of insanity from Miss Yoder's name altogether. It was not going to be easy, in fact Reid didn't think it had ever been done—though that could be down to no one having ever tried.

'I have only good intentions, Miss Yoder, I'll see you tomorrow.' He smiled again and stood. 'Your brother says to make sure you remember to turn the taps off.'

The next afternoon, after failing to keep a low profile in order to avoid being observed by Dr. Reid, Alice was escorted to his office by one of the nurses. As she entered the room, Dr. Reid looked up and smiled.

'Good afternoon Alice, may I call you Alice?'

Alice nodded.

'Thank you; and I of course extend the same courtesy—you can call me Jim.'

Alice did not say anything, but sat when he gestured to the chair opposite his.

'What happened to your lip?' he inquired, noticing the swelling and discolouration.

When Alice did not answer, the nurse in the doorway huffed.

'She got into a fight this morning during wash time,' the nurse explained, sounding unimpressed.

'Yes, yes, thank you Mildred. You aren't required to sit in on this observation, so you may leave to your other duties now.' Dr. Reid dismissed her with a wave of his hand, still looking at Alice with such curiosity that had he been a cat, he would have dropped dead to the floor. The door clicked shut.

'So, Alice, my plan so far is to observe you—for a little longer than normal—and then hopefully determine a new diagnosis and argue to the board that your current diagnosis should be officially changed. Best case scenario, they deem you capable of being released but bear in mind this has never happened before as far as I know. Worst case scenario, they tell me to bugger off.'

He could see her expression change as she clearly mulled over his words, but she still made no attempt to converse with him. He knew it would be impossible to prove her intelligence and understanding without speech. After musing over the situation for a few moments, Jim recollected part of his conversation with Leonard in the dimly lit pub. The young man had spoken fondly of his sister, and he had also mentioned her love of books.

His eyes focused back on the room around him, and settled back onto Alice. Hers flicked back up to the ceiling. *She had been observing the observer;* he just about succeeded in not chuckling at himself.

'Do you like books?' he enquired, his tone as nonchalant as he could make it.

Alice's eyes snapped to his for a second before returning to the ceiling. Jim could see that she was counting the tiles from the ways her eyes were scanning. He noted this down quite positively.

'If you talk with me, I could bring you some books to read?' He changed his tone to make the offer sound appealing, but he was aware that it sounded more like he was trying to convince a small child to behave by bribing them with sweets.

Alice hesitated, but eventually said, 'I don't respond to blackmail, Jim.'

Jim laughed loudly, reveling in the sound of the young girl's voice. He rifled through his desk draws a moment, looking for a medical journal he knew he had left in there.

'This probably won't interest you, but it should keep your attention until I can bring you a book of your choosing.' He smiled, handing her the heavy book.

She took it, and Jim thought she looked fragile, as if she was going to crumple under its weight, but her arms were strong and she held it steady.

'Thank you,' she whispered.

Dr. Jim Reid grinned. *Progress*, he thought.

Over the next few weeks, Dr. Reid met with Alice every afternoon and encouraged her to talk to him. She would talk when it suited her, but other than that, no steps forward were really made. Alice would sometimes complain about the drugs that she was given. They were crushed into her food after her resistance to taking them orally, and because of this she was no longer eating much. She would reflect on her observations: she had noticed the patients were given drugs that made them docile, not better. Dr. Reid had dismissed this idea when she had mentioned it and tried to avoid the puncture wounds scattered across Alice's arms, but he knew that this was the unfortunate truth. There had also been occasions where Alice had gotten into fights when other patients had invaded her personal space.

The breakthrough did not come until one night when the blond doctor was reading an article on Autism and the work of Hans Asperger. The disorder itself was a fairly new term, and it was not something he was familiar with. However, as he read the symptoms—withdrawn, social impairments, above average intelligence, linked to schizophrenia—he immediately related these with Alice's behavior. He proceeded to stay up until the early hours of the morning, researching as much as he could.

Arranging a meeting with the board was not an easy feat, but Jim finally managed it two weeks after he had first read the article. He walked into the office with an air of confidence, his step not faltering even when he saw Dr. Hunter sitting at the table opposite the three men he would be trying to convince to release Alice.

'Good morning, gentlemen.' Dr. Reid smiled warmly at the men, shaking each of their hands as they uttered their less than cheerful replies.

They were wealthy and powerful men, all of them guilty of cutting corners to save money or exploit as many people as they could get away with. Reid was hoping to appeal to their compassionate sides. He had his work cut out for him. They were the top of the hierarchy at Greymore, and their word was final.

'Dr. Hunter, I wasn't informed you were going to be attending?' Reid queried subtly.

'Well, I have to defend myself against your ridiculous claims about my diagnostic abilities,' Hunter sneered.

'Don't be difficult, Norman,' Reid chastised.

Dr. Hunter scoffed, and was about to retort when one of the men on the other side of the table cleared his throat loudly.

'Dr. Reid, if you don't mind, we all have places to be, so let's get straight to the point, please?' Blanton's subcutaneous fat around his chin wobbled as he spoke, and Reid had a hard time taking the committee chairman seriously.

'Of course Sir,' Reid smiled. 'I believe one of the patients at Greymore, Miss Alice Yoder, has received an incorrect diagnosis. To rectify this, I am of the opinion that she be released and sent to a foster home so that she may receive the correct treatment for her condition.'

'And what condition is *that*, Dr. Reid?' snapped Fraser, his almost toothless mouth twisted into a look of annoyance.

'I believe she has a condition called Autism Syndrome Disorder, or a more recent variation currently being explored by Hans Asperger.'

Dr. Hunter exploded immediately. 'This is outrageous! You're undermining my diagnosis, and I've no doubt that you made that "Assburger" fellow up!'

Dr. Reid stifled a laugh. *'Asperger,* Norman,' he corrected 'and no, I haven't made it up—perhaps if you indulged in contemporary reading . . . ?'

The question was rhetorical, so when Hunter opened his mouth to answer he turned his back and proceeded to place the articles on the table in front of the three vultures. They peered at them, trying to seem blasé to the fact they were reading the work of a German doctor.

'And the cause of Autism, it says here, is lack of affection received during the developmental stages?' Dr. Temple inquired.

'Yes Sir, a more common term is having had a "refrigerator mother". The best treatment to date is for the sufferer to be sent to a foster home.' Reid smiled; Temple was his best shot for the sympathy vote as he had a handful of children whom he secretly adored.

'Dr. Hunter, how *did* you establish such a specific diagnosis so quickly?' Dr. Temple turned his attention to Hunter, raising one thick grey eyebrow.

'Her lack of speech informs us of her mental retardation, her violent episode in which she gave me a periorbital hematoma is a clear sign of schizophrenic behavior, and her inability to maintain eye contact suggests she is self-absorbed.' Hunter puffed out his chest with pride at his diagnosis.

Dr. Reid interjected, 'I have spoken to both nurses who sat in on your observation, and both Marjory and

Eleanor reported that Miss Yoder's "violent episode" was provoked, and more an act of self-defense than anything else. Her selectively mute behavior is the most common trait presented in Autistic children. Miss Yoder also confided in me that you stared at her bare chest after you'd had her strapped to the bed in the padded room for almost an entire day, during which she was neither fed nor hydrated. But we'll skip over that, shall we?' Reid had been furious when Alice had mentioned this, and so he had planned to mention it if things were not going his way in order to sway the board's decision. They would not want to fire Dr. Hunter, so they would have to agree to his terms.

Hunter's eyes bulged. Not only had the patient *spoken*, but she had also been more aware than he had imagined. Of course, it was his word against that of an insane child, but it was still cause for concern.

'Calm yourself down, Jim.' Temple raised his hand in an attempt to keep the peace. 'Dr. Hunter,' he continued, 'an investigation will be required regarding this incident should Miss Yoder continue to be a patient at this facility. I'm assuming that is something you don't wish to happen?' Dr. Temple concluded; the distaste heavy in his tone.

Dr. Hunter hung his head and dropped his shoulders. 'No, Sir,' he muttered, his hands balled into fists.

'Then you will have to withdraw your diagnosis and Dr. Reid, we will need a report of your diagnosis and all logged observation time. I assume this report is already written?' Temple smiled slightly as Reid nodded. 'Right, my only concern, Dr. Reid, is that finding a foster home suitable could take months, even years.'

'I have already organised the foster home, Sir, a woman named Julia Fenton. She's had a number of autistic children in her home before, all of whom have gone on to be capable, independent people,' Reid explained, trying not to convey his pleasure at things having gone his way.

'Then it's settled, unless either of you have anything to add?' Temple turned to the other two men, both of whom shook their heads. They had not really cared to begin with.

'Excellent, the necessary paperwork can be filled out this week and then the patient can be discharged on Friday.'

With those final words, the three men stood, shook hands with Dr. Reid, glared at Dr. Hunter for forcing them into such a position, bid goodbye and left the room. Reid tried not to look too smug as he followed them out.

'Now, Alice, there are only two rules in my house. If you want something, you have to ask for it, and you must say please and thank you when appropriate. I won't force you to speak at any other time, ok?' Ms Fenton smiled warmly.

Alice nodded, deciding that this seemed reasonable.

'Brilliant, and please, call me Julia.'

Julia Fenton was a tall woman with long blonde hair twisted up into a bun. She had bright green eyes and a constant smile. Alice liked her hair. Jon, the young boy that was also living in the house was only ten. Alice thought Jon had big ears, but he seemed okay, especially as he was quiet too. He had hidden behind Julia when Alice had arrived, and whispered a simple hello before giggling and running back to his room. He was light on his feet, so he didn't even make a lot of noise while running up the stairs. Alice decided that living with pretty Julia and quiet Jon was one hundred percent better than Greymore.

Leonard had hardly been able to wait to visit Alice after going out to celebrate with Dr. Reid on the evening of the board meeting. He had brought as many of Alice's clothes and books as he could carry. He knocked on the door and was met by a very delicate looking woman, no older than thirty. He smiled widely.

'Hello, I'm Leonard, Alice's brother. You must be Ms. Fenton. I've brought some of my sister's things,' he explained. 'Dr. Reid said that it would be ok?' He smiled hopefully, and the woman beamed at him.

'Of course, come in. She's been eager to see you, I can tell.' She beckoned him inside the small house.

He put the bag of books down heavily by the stairs and shrugged the satchel off his shoulder.

'Alice?' Julia called, though soft footsteps could already be heard coming down the stairs.

'Hey Alice, just thought I'd come see how my favourite sister was doing.' Leonard grinned, tears filling his eyes at the first sight of his sister in what had been too long.

'I'm your only sister, Leonard.' Alice smiled widely, opening her arms for a hug.

Leonard hesitated for only a second, in pure shock at this new gesture, but then he quickly swooped down and wrapped his arms around her, hugging tight.

'God, I'm glad you're out of that bloody place,' he murmured.

Alice did not reply, but stepped out of the embrace shortly afterwards.

'I knew you would fix it like you promised,' she said softly, smiling at her brother again as she looked into his eyes and then down. 'That is a new shirt.'

He laughed. *Yeah, Alice is going to be just fine.*

1950–60s

AND THE DENIAL OF ATTRACTION

MY THROAT BURNED. The bile that was being forced out of my stomach ripped my oesophagus as my body folded and lurched forward. The picture I had been shown was of a pretty woman, and I had been told to look at her closely. I was asked if I found her attractive, to which I shamefully nodded before Doctor Gunn pushed his fingers down past my tonsils. This time I could feel it come out of my nose as well, which stung like a bitch. The procedure was repeated for what felt like days, with a new picture being used each time. Dr. Gunn stopped when there was nothing left in my stomach to bring up.

By the end of the session, my windpipe was raw and the smell of sick clung to my nostrils. I hoarsely thanked the seemingly solemn doctor, who nodded briefly.

'Same time next week, Miss Darling,' he added, before turning back to his notes.

I headed back to the day room, gently touching my sore throat. I had admitted myself into Greymore almost a month ago, and for this reason I was something of a leper amongst the other patients who were here against their will. While I was not too concerned about making friends, their lack of acceptance made me feel even more isolated. I could not understand it, honestly. We were all here to be treated, so it was a mystery to me why whenever I walked into a room, a cloud of silence immediately descended.

I made a detour, stepping inside the washroom to try and soothe the burning in my throat and wash the smell of vomit out of my nose. There were no mirrors anywhere on the ward, due to suicide and injury risks, so I cannot describe what I looked like, though I could make an educated guess and say "horrendous". I turned on a tap— they were all cold—at one of the basins and splashed some water on my face, blowing my nose into the sink before swallowing icy mouthfuls. The force of gulping pried pieces of loose flesh from my damaged throat, and I almost gagged again. Finally, I splashed my face once more and then dried it with the bottom of my rather unflattering plain white Greymore issued t-shirt.

I continued on my way to the day room, and found my thoughts drifting to Vivian before I could stop myself. The look on her face when I had told her that my mother had suggested I admit myself into Greymore had almost been enough for me to scrap the whole idea; she had looked devastated. But then her expression had changed to one I knew well—the same look crossed her face when she was protesting.

'Cat,' she had said, exasperated from across the room, 'liking women is not a bloody disease!' Her hands had gestured wildly in frustration. 'It's a part of you, and you need to accept that about yourself, you can't be cured of something that isn't wrong in the first place!'

'I have to try, Viv. My mother thinks I'm trying to show her up with my bohemian lifestyle.' I had started crying then. 'It's your fault for pushing me to tell them!'

Viv looked hurt for a moment before her jaw set.

'You can't just change to be who your mother wants you to be. If you did, you wouldn't be living your life, you'd be living a shell of a life.'

I sighed. 'Come with me?' I pleaded.

'I'm sure as hell not going to a nuthouse. There's nothing wrong with who I am.' Vivian had scoffed.

'*Society thinks there is, though!*' I blurted.

'*Society doesn't think women are even capable of loving other women!*' she had protested. '*Plus society changes its mind all the time. Women can vote now, for crying out loud. Society will change its mind about homos too, soon enough.*'

I had left, and the next day I admitted myself into Greymore. I knew it was wrong to miss her, but I did. I could almost hear my mother's voice scolding me for such thoughts, but I could not help it.

I sulked into the day room and rolled my eyes at the silence that fell, grumbling about how the women in the room clearly had nothing better to talk about. I slumped into one of the chairs in the corner, not pointed at anything in particular, and took the pills that the nurse gave me without argument. I swallowed them without water; a skill I had developed since coming here. They were a little harder to take this afternoon due to the state of my throat, and I winced as I felt them go down. I then returned to my thoughts before the drowsiness could hit me.

I had met Vivian at a bar that I had heard was for people like me. She had walked over with a confidence I could not—and still cannot—understand. I had repeatedly talked myself out of even setting foot into the bar, and it was five attempts before I actually made it in. So when she asked me if I wanted to dance I had spluttered my drink down my particularly nice and very new white summer dress. At this point realization dawned on her face.

'*Oh, first time here?*'

I had nodded and turned a deep shade of red, though thankfully no one could tell because of the poor lighting. She had sighed and turned to walk away, but then with an assertiveness I had not known I possessed, I grabbed her wrist.

'I would like to dance,' I had murmured.

She had made several comments as we danced about how she should not get involved with someone who clearly was not comfortable with themselves, since it could only go tits up. But we had been together for almost two years since that night, when she invited me up to her flat near the bar.

Looking back, despite the arguments about my self-loathing, or her not understanding my hesitations in being open, we were happy. When I eventually did tell my parents—after Viv's persuasions—it did not make things better between us as I had believed it would.

My eyes focused back on the room around me, and I dabbed at my damp cheeks.

'What's wrong, Darling; couldn't quite throw up the gay today?' Bertha, one of the more masculine women goaded.

She had had it in for me since she had found out I was here voluntarily. I ignored her, blinking back fresh tears. I didn't know how she knew about my most recent therapy session, but then I wasn't exactly quiet when retching up my insides, and in hindsight, I suppose she and I had similar treatment.

'Leave the poor woman alone, Butch.' The voice was unfamiliar, and through watery eyes I looked for the source.

A new girl, young looking, no older than eighteen, walked towards me with a tentative smile on her face. She sat on the chair opposite, her back facing the rest of the room. She had shoulder-length blonde hair and green eyes. Her frame was slim, her arms toned but not overly muscular, and she had tanned skin, as though she had spent a lot of time outdoors.

'Were you just checking me out?' she asked, grinning.

I felt my cheeks go hot. 'No!' I objected, apparently not too convincingly because she started laughing.

'I don't mind. You aren't so bad looking yourself . . . considering your age.' She winked provocatively, and I gaped.

'I'm only twenty-eight!' I declared, trying to defend my looks, though I was aware that my time at Greymore had aged me by about ten years.

'Don't have a cow, I was only joking.' She smiled, this time it was friendly as opposed to teasing; an attempt to make amends. 'Anyway, why was Butch giving you trouble? Did you sleep with her and then not call?'

I laughed, and was amazed by how unaccustomed I was to it. I quickly sobered up at my impending answer.

'She gives me trouble because I'm here voluntarily,' I muttered quickly, but apparently the young blonde had hawk ears.

'Ah, the denial phase; got to love it.' Her indifference shocked me; every other person in here treated me like I had the plague. She, however, seemed more empathetic.

'You don't think I'm pathetic for trying to be normal?' I asked, completely bewildered.

'Not pathetic,' she smiled, 'just naïve. I'm Melinda, by the way.' She held out a hand for me to shake.

'I'm Catherine,' I started before registering her previous comment. 'What do you mean: "naïve"?' I sounded more defensive than I had intended.

'I meant no offence. Well, not much. I was just saying you've clearly fallen for the shit that the idiots running the country use to convince everyone that being queer is an illness and a sin. I mean, think about it: *straight* people decided being queer is a mental illness. Why should *they* get to decide that without being questioned? There have been same sex couples since before "Jesus",' she made quotation marks with her fingers, 'when two guys shared a pyramid in Egypt. I had a cat that was queer, for God's sake. I came downstairs and found him spooning another tom-cat; my point is, no one tried to "cure" him.'

Apparently Melinda had ranted a little too loudly, because then the Head Nurse, clearly rattled, called for the evening medication to be handed out half an hour early. We all dutifully swallowed our pills. It didn't take long for the people in the room to become subdued and the edges of my vision to become blurred.

'Bloody hell, what did they give us?' Melinda asked, sounding a little vacant.

'No idea, but you get used to it. Kind of.' My reply was slurred.

I watched the shadows move along the floor, slowly, and the light that shone in turned orange as the sun set. Without knowing who got up first or what signal was given, we all shuffled out of the day room and into our sleeping quarters. By some miracle, Melinda was allocated the empty bed next to mine and she grinned at me, winking as she got changed. I diverted my eyes and crawled into bed, the pills knocking me out as if on cue.

'So, how did you end up being admitted here?' I was curious, since in the two weeks she had been here, we had only really talked about me.

'Ah,' Melinda faltered, scratching the back of her neck, 'my parents had me sectioned.'

'How?' I exclaimed.

'I'm only seventeen; I guess they figured they should do something about me while they still could.' She laughed awkwardly, shuffling the breakfast around the plate she was hunched over.

'Wow, now I feel *really* old,' I groaned, and then mentally reprimanded myself for not being more sympathetic. 'I'm really sorry; I can't imagine what that must be like . . .'

Melinda laughed more genuinely. 'Yeah, because it's *oh so different* to your mom bullying you into admitting yourself.'

I reeled. 'My mother didn't bully me. She encouraged me to come here to help me be happy!' I knew I sounded ridiculously defensive, but it was true.

'Her definition of happy, or yours Cath?' Melinda raised an eyebrow as if she knew the answer.

I exhaled sharply, leaving my breakfast plate and grumbling a quick goodbye before storming out of the dining hall, not unlike a child.

'Think about it Cath!' she called after me.

Despite my best efforts, I went into the treatment room still thinking about what Melinda had said. So much so, that I wasn't listening to what Dr. Gunn was saying and just nodded at what seemed to be the right moments. This, as well as the fact that the nurses gave everyone their pills a little later than usual, which meant I was feeling a little vacant, resulted in me being caught completely off guard when I was led to the room I had overheard the other women describe.

I was seated and Dr. Gunn asked one of the nurses to attach the equipment to me. My breath hitched. Since there were very few women in Greymore, it was impossible, even for an outcast such as me, to not know everyone. So when Joanne had come out of one of her sessions and couldn't remember what a spoon was for, it hadn't taken long for the rest of us to discover that the doctors had tried to "electrify it out of her".

I could feel beads of sweat collecting on my forehead; I had a ridiculously low pain threshold, and I didn't want to forget how to wipe my own behind. *Oh god, what if I forget more important things—memories? What if I forget about Viv?* A tear rolled down my cheek at that possibility. *But isn't that what you're here for?*

I was told there would be an electric shock each time a woman appeared on the screen. I swallowed hard, my still damaged throat stinging a little.

I will not forget.

I could feel my breathing become more rapid as the nurse approached me with a syringe. Within minutes, I was cut off. It felt as though my body was dead, but my consciousness had remained in my corpse.

I will not forget.

My heart increased its rhythm; to the point that I thought it was a heart attack. I tried to scream, to tell the doctor that something was wrong, by my jaw would not move, the words were lost on my tongue.

I will not forget.

It was dark outside when I staggered back into the day room, exhausted physically and mentally. Melinda was sat in what had become our corner, gazing at a random spot on the wall, a frown creasing her otherwise smooth face. She had a newspaper open on her lap, no doubt a few days old. As I slumped into the chair opposite her—the one she had sat in almost two weeks ago—I groaned, the feeling of nausea turning my stomach. I did not want to be sick again, the enamel on my teeth was already fighting a losing battle and my gums were becoming infected. Melinda shot a fleeting glance in my direction before returning to the spot on the wall. I rolled my eyes, the gesture causing a sharp pain to echo through my head.

'Okay, so you may have been right earlier . . .' I started, my voice sounding foreign, distant.

'About what?' Melinda prompted, raising an eyebrow.

I sighed. Telling a seventeen year old they are right about something probably wasn't the best of ideas, and it wasn't something I was used to: being wrong. Or rather, *admitting* I was wrong. More pressing, however, was the frustration I felt due to the lack of control over my lips and tongue.

'About my mother . . .' I managed, 'wanting what's best for her and not me.'

'It's about damn time!'

I rolled my eyes again at her ridiculous teenage confidence. *I'm not even that sure of myself now, let alone ten years ago . . .* Another shooting pain exploded in my temples and my vision overlapped, creating two of everything in sight. I frowned, pinching the bridge of my nose.

'What's wrong, Cath?' Melinda's smug look turned to one of concern.

'Well, I just had the shock of my life,' I snickered, trying to make light of the situation.

'Why? What happened?' Melinda asked, clearly missing my genius word play.

'You know, for someone as wise beyond their years as you, you are rather slow—and coming from *me* that's saying something.' I laughed, ignoring her objection. 'I meant that I had my brain fried . . . electron-something . . . fried like an egg.'

'God Cath, are you alright?' She leaned forward as if to check for visible damage. 'What's your name? What do you use a spoon for?' Melinda asked without pausing for breath. 'Also, both those jokes were awful.'

I laughed hysterically, throwing my head back. My cackling caused people—especially the nurses—to look over with irritated expressions, so I inhaled deeply in an attempt to calm myself down. 'I'm fine,' I dismissed once the room stopped spinning. 'What's in the paper?' I asked, suddenly interested in the odd letters across its pages.

Melinda looked at me, concerned for a moment before picking the paper up off her lap and handing it to me.

'The protestor with the "people with closed minds should close their mouths" sign is gorgeous.' She grinned, wiggling her eyebrows at me.

I giggled like a teenager doing something they know they shouldn't, and then looked at the picture she was referring too. The woman looked familiar, and I could have sworn I knew her from somewhere, but for the life of me I couldn't remember where.

'She is very pretty,' I agreed, which caused Melinda to laugh. 'What?' I asked, self-consciously looking down at myself.

'Nothing.' She tried to collect herself. 'Just that the electricity clearly didn't help; I mean you're practically salivating over that picture.'

'Actually, I think that may be because I currently have little control over my tongue,' I retorted.

'Oh really?' Melinda raised her eyebrows, teasing and full of innuendo. 'Clearly Greymore's master plan is to make lesbians completely useless in bed.'

I threw the newspaper at her, causing us both to laugh like mad women.

I was sat in the day room, doing one of the jigsaws that had about sixteen missing pieces, when Bertha strolled in looking smug.

'So Darling, what are you going to do once your girlfriend is gone?' she mocked.

I frowned. 'What are you talking about?'

Apparently this was a better reaction than she had been expecting because she guffawed.

'You don't know? Your girlfriend is packing her things.'

I stopped breathing for a moment. I had not really acknowledged how dependent I had become on Melinda since her arrival, but I was feeling the force of it now with the prospect of her leaving.

'But she can't be leaving, she'd have told me,' I murmured to myself. *Then again,* I thought, *my memory hasn't exactly been up to scratch the last few days. But surely I wouldn't forget her telling me something so important?* I could hear my blood pumping in my ears.

Bertha rolled her eyes. 'Go and see for yourself if you don't believe me.'

I half didn't want to, partially because I didn't want her to think I had doubts, and partially because I didn't want her to be right. But I stood, slowly—I had started getting shooting pains in my head and lower back when I stood too quickly—and headed towards the bedrooms. I ignored Bertha's ill-formed taunts as I left, and almost staggered into the sleeping quarters as a pain seared up my back. I un-scrunched my eyes and immediately wished I hadn't. Melinda was tossing her clothes into a small brown suitcase with a careless impatience.

'What are you doing?' I murmured, barely above a whisper.

Melinda sighed heavily, dropping the socks she had been holding, exasperated.

'My parents came to see me this morning, asking me if I had learnt my lesson.' She forced a sarcastic laugh.

I selfishly thought of my own parents. They hadn't come to visit once since I had been admitted, and the irony was almost too much. I had put myself through this hell to be a better daughter for them, but they hadn't made the effort to come and see me even once. I blinked.

'What happened?' I asked, moving to sit on the bed, though it was nowhere near as graceful as I would have liked.

Melinda rolled her eyes at my lack of elegance, fighting a smile, and threw a dark red t-shirt at me in jest. I pulled it off my head and clutched it to my chest, running my other hand through my hair in an attempt to smooth it back down.

'They wanted me to agree to marry some idiot,' she spat out, clearly disgusted.

I choked on air, struggling not to laugh. The idea of Melinda getting married to a man was a humorous one. She was just too . . . *proud of being gay.*

'So what did you say?' I asked.

'I said yes.'

I felt numb. Melinda had been gone for two weeks, and I had fallen into a deep depression. I barely ate, and I had once again become withdrawn and introverted. I was majorly pissed at the young blonde. She had continuously lectured me about accepting myself and not being ashamed—to the point that I was actually starting to convert to her way of thinking—and then she shows her lack of backbone and goes off to get bloody *married*. In short, I felt betrayed. Despite the age gap, Melinda was my friend, and though I hated to admit it, she had given me hope that being gay was okay. This revelation, however, had been shattered the moment she had left. For the two days after she revealed to me that she was leaving, I'd convinced myself it was a joke; that she wasn't really going to marry some chauvinistic prat. There may also be a slight chance that I was a little bit jealous. But then she had left.

Melinda had approached me in the sleeping quarters almost timidly, and under different circumstances this alone would have caused me to laugh.

'So, I'm leaving now, Cath, my parents are waiting in reception.'

I turned my back to her, aware that I was being childish but unable to find it in me to care. She had no doubt rolled her eyes before wrapping her arms around my shoulders in a tight hug. I was shifting out of the embrace when her lips crashed into mine. The kiss wasn't one of romance, it was brief: reassuring. After another fleeting kiss to my temple, she left the room, waving awkwardly before stepping out of the doorway and down the hall.

What the hell just happened?

I was shook from my thoughts by one of the nurses tapping my shoulder. I ignored the almost repulsed look on her face, as if the gay was contagious.

'You have a letter, Miss Darling,' she muttered.

'Thank you Nurse. You're too kind.' I smiled sweetly, deliberately brushing my hand against hers as I took the letter—if only to entertain myself.

When she walked away a little too briskly, I rolled my eyes and tucked the letter into the waistband of my trousers before returning to stare blankly at the food in front of me. It wasn't until later that afternoon that I took out the letter to read. I had not received any contact attempts from the world outside of Greymore since I admitted myself, so I was more than a little eager as I tore the envelope and pulled out the paper. I flipped the page and was startled to find it was from Melinda.

> *Cath,*
>
> *I have sent you two copies of this letter—one to Greymore and one to your home address in the hopes that you might have signed yourself out of that god awful place. So wherever you are reading this from, I just want to say I'm sorry for leaving the way I did. I'm also sorry for lying to you, but I had to be cautious about telling you what I'm about to tell you in case one of the idiot nurses or patients overheard. I'm running away. When my parents asked me if I would marry what's-his-name, I said yes so that I would be able to leave Greymore and then leave before the never-going-to-happen wedding. I'm actually writing this from the airport. I hope you aren't mad at me, and if you are, I ask that you understand my situation and forgive me for leaving like a tosser. I'm going to go to America, and you had better come and visit me once you've won your woman back! I hate to say it, but I'm almost glad I ended up in Greymore, because it meant that we met, and you're not too bad. What I'm trying to say is: I hope we're still friends, and I hope you write back. I've put a return address on a separate piece of*

paper—it's a P.O. Box for until I find a permanent place.

Love always,
Melinda

P.S. I put the newspaper with the gorgeous protestor under your mattress.
P.P.S. I'm hoping my English accent will help me out with the American ladies.
P.P.P.S. Not that you *aren't a good kisser, but that was a friend thing. I hope that was clear.*

I tried and failed to suppress my snickering at the end of the letter, and I couldn't help but feel guilty for my emotions over the past few weeks. The thought of Melinda, the now-eighteen year old, in America on her own, reignited the protectiveness I felt towards her. America was huge. Melinda was 5'3 at most. My eyes flicked over the letter again, faltering on *"once you've won your woman back!"* Realising that it had been a long time since I had thought about Viv, I tried to picture her face and found that I couldn't. Tears flooded my eyes and spilt onto the letter, blurring some of the words on the page. Dabbing at the blotches, I looked back at Melinda's elegant scrawl and laughed at her postscripts, reaching under the mattress for the newspaper. I only had vague recollections of the evening after my first and last electro-shock therapy session, and could barely remember throwing the newspaper at a hysterical Melinda. This is why, when I retrieved the crumpled pages I was stunned to recognize that it had been Viv that Melinda and I had fawned over so distastefully. *Apparently I think she's beautiful even when*

I can't recognize her, I thought, *and it's a little worrying that Melinda and I have a similar taste in women.* I forced a smile, humouring myself to detract from the fact that I had forgotten what Vivian had looked like, even when presented with a picture of her.

Becoming conscious of the fact that the "gorgeous protestor" was Viv, I read the story associated with her picture, and learned that she had been protesting for gay rights in what was being described as a copycat riot; similar to some happening in America.

Clarity struck me; being in Greymore where I was trying and failing to deny who I am, with people constantly telling me that I'm going through a phase, was making me miserable. I realized that the people I knew—namely Viv and Melinda—that don't give a shit about other people's opinions, were happy. Genuinely happy. As I glanced down again at Viv's picture, I understood that the problem between us had mostly been me. I had wanted to be "normal", and hadn't even tried to hide it. My stomach churned at the idea of how that must have made Vivian feel. Becoming overwhelmed with guilt, my eyes welled with tears and my throat felt constricted. I had forced Vivian back into the closet for the duration of our relationship, and the fact that I was only just realising the fault in my actions appalled me.

I signed myself out of Greymore that afternoon. *I have to win my woman back,* I thought, echoing the words of Melinda's letter. *Or at the very least, apologise.*

Vivian was on the side of the road, along with a substantial group of both men and women. The group was standing outside of the local police station, where some of their friends were reportedly being held as a result of a previous protest. They were all holding cardboard protest signs. She was in her element, yet she kept clutching at her hair or pinching the bridge of her nose. The people around her had formed a tight unit, making any attempts to separate them or even physical assault more difficult. However, Vivian frowned as she saw the people on the front line separating into two halves.

'Hello stranger.'

Vivian's eyes widened at the sound of my voice, and she shifted her sign so she could look at me. Her eyes revealed her shock at seeing me standing in the middle of her protest. She stood, as if unsure of how to proceed or what to do with herself. I wrung my hands nervously.

'What are you doing here, Cat?' she finally murmured with a slight scowl on her face, as though preparing for a confrontation.

'Okay . . .' I started, to which she raised an eyebrow. I sighed, and unbuttoned my knee-length coat to reveal a white sundress—the one I was wearing when we first met. Now, it was customised with black paint, though my handwriting left something to be desired. It read: *I am queer.*

'I'm doing whatever it takes, whatever you need or want me to do to show you—hell, to show everyone—that I love you Viv. I'm just sorry I had to be such an idiot before I realised it.' The declaration was one I had planned since I had started painting over the cotton material, and I could see Viv was struggling to remain indifferent; her cheeks had gained colour and she exhaled sharply through her nose.

Through pursed lips, she retorted 'Have you completely lost your mind?'

'Ironically, I think I found it somewhere amongst the craziness of Greymore.' I smiled, trying to ease the tension between us. I knew I'd hurt her, and I hadn't expected to be welcomed back into her life with unquestioning and open arms, but I had no intention of giving up.

'Cat, you've been gone for months . . .' she looked down at the pavement, averting her eyes from my gaze. 'You can't just . . . I can't . . . I've . . .' she stuttered.

I suppressed a giggle at the gorgeous protestor, usually so fiery and confident, being unable to get her thoughts across.

'Are you seeing anyone?' I asked bluntly. It was the only question I needed an answer to.

'No,' the woman I had stupidly pushed away responded.

'Then nothing else matters to me other than you giving me another chance,' I declared.

Viv scoffed, folding her arms over her chest defensively. I closed the space between us and kissed her, trying to prove that I meant what I had been saying. That I had changed. Abruptly, there were forearms pushing me away. It was unusual being on the receiving end of such actions, after being the one to implement them for so long. Hazel eyes seemed to search my own, and then hands were on my face, pulling me back towards her, brushing her lips against mine. I giggled like a love struck teenager, and the people around us were clapping and whooping.

'Shut up,' she whispered, 'I'm still pissed at you.' The tone of her voice betrayed her, but I didn't comment.

I'd won my woman back.

AND THE FRIENDS OF DOROTHY

THE WOMAN WAS pretty. She was "look over your shoulder to do a double-take" pretty, and yet Clive merely nodded politely as he stood next to her, before he turned to the barman and ordered his round.

'Do I get one too?' she asked, placing her delicate hand on the forearm that he was resting on the bar.

Clive looked at the hand on his arm, then at the woman. His thick brown eyebrows rose in surprise. He was being flirted with. He cleared his throat, glancing at his table of friends, and Peter. Peter, with his thick red hair and blue eyes, was laughing at something George was saying.

'You have a drink right there.' Clive smiled slightly, gesturing to the full wine glass in front of her.

'You caught me.' She held her hands up as though surrendering. 'But it got us talking. I'm Evelyn.'

'Clive Hart.'

'So you're here with friends?'

'Yes,' he says, glancing back at the table. Peter was looking over at him now, an eyebrow raised. 'Just some friends,' he said as he turned back to her. 'I really ought to get back to them.'

He paid the barman and picked up his tray of drinks.

'It was nice to meet you though.' Clive smiled again politely, before moving back over to the table.

'You too,' Evelyn whispered to the now empty space.

Clive placed the tray on the table before sitting back down next to Tom.

'You'll never guess what just happened . . .' he interrupted the current conversation on how awful George was in the kitchen.

The men at the table turned to him expectantly. George's green eyes sparkled, having glanced over during Clive's exchange with the woman. Tom ran a hand through his curly brown hair to get some of it out of his face, and Peter looked at him from his place across the table, his foot resting on top of Clive's.

'That woman over there was just flirting with me.'

The men all turned to look at where their friend was gesturing.

'Don't all look at once!' Clive hissed.

George glanced first, then swatted at Tom's hand for his turn. Peter casually looked over his shoulder.

'She's a looker,' Tom exclaimed. 'Did you tell her she wasn't your type?' He laughed.

Clive chuckled with him. 'Not in so many words. I just said I had to get back over here.'

'To your sexy man lover?' George finished, smirking.

Clive laughed, but shook his head. Peter squinted at him.

'You didn't tell her you're with me?' he asked.

'I didn't need too.' Clive smiled slightly, shrugging it off.

Peter gave an unimpressed scoff before picking his drink out of the recently brought round and drinking the whole thing.

Clive suspected he was in trouble.

They had not stayed much longer. Clive had attempted to act normally with his friends, but Peter's obvious frustration was causing an awkward mist to sit over their table. Most noticeable had been when Tom was recounting a story he had heard about one of his friends from school being admitted into Greymore—the local institute—for drug abuse. He had become really sick, and his family didn't suspect he would make it to the end of the year. Both George and Clive had reacted accordingly, offering sympathy and commenting on how awful Greymore was as a place to attempt to redeem one's health in. All eyes had turned to Peter for his input, only to be met with a halfhearted nod of agreement.

Clive sighed, and then leaned across to Peter.

'Would you like to go?'

Peter shrugged, but stood to leave.

Peter's front door clicked softly behind them, and Clive draped his coat over the back of the sofa and stood awkwardly, pulling at his ear lobe. He opened his mouth to say something, but was interrupted before he could even begin.

'So, she was pretty.' Peter said from across the room.

Clive frowned, trying to remember the woman's face.

'I guess so,' he finally responded.

Peter scoffed. 'You're the one who occasionally likes women, you should know.'

Clive clenched his jaw. 'That's hardly fair; you're the one who spends all day with a bunch of actors who fall all over themselves around you!'

'Oh please!' Peter rolled his eyes as he poured himself a drink, his hat and coat resting on the arm of the chair near him. 'Why didn't you just tell her?' he asks finally as he picks them up and places them onto the hooks by the front door.

'You live in theatre land, Peter, where people have been out for years—but in the real world, we still need to be careful.' Clive threw his hands up. 'Besides, it didn't seem necessary!'

Peter pulled at his dark red hair, exasperated. 'If I were a woman, you would have told her!' he argued.

Though Peter loved Clive, he was—a lot of the time—worried that he would lose him to the easier option of a woman, since Clive had admitted early on that he was attracted to both men and women. Usually, it was something Peter forgot, due to the feminine swish of Clive's hips and the amount of time he spent with their few queer friends.

'If you were a woman, I'd have a thousand less problems!' Clive shouted, and Peter's expression was enough to make him immediately regret it. He rubbed his face, pushing his glasses up onto his forehead, as if trying to wipe away his words. 'Bollocks, Peter, I didn't mean that-' he started, but was quickly interrupted.

'But you did.' Peter was fighting the welling of his eyes. 'I think you should leave Clive. If women are so much easier, then . . .' he trailed off, throwing his hands up as though even he wasn't sure what his point was.

'But . . . Peter, I . . .' Clive wasn't sure how to respond; though he was sure saying anything was better than spluttering.

Peter sighed, as if resigning himself.

'You need to figure things out, Clive. I think we both do. But I won't wait forever.'

Clive was fighting his own tears now. He hated that he had used Peter's fears to goad him, but being at a complete loss for words meant he could only nod, pick up his coat from the back of the sofa and flee.

*　　*　　*

Clive pulled his coat tighter around himself. The cool evening air was harsh and he rubbed his hands together in the hopes of generating some warmth. He turned and took a breath before walking into the pub.

They had first come to this pub for one of its secret "homo friendly" evenings, though it was a safe place to have a drink on most other nights as well. The owners, a married couple, were undoubtedly just trying to bring in extra customers, but they were also decent in making sure all their patrons were free from harassment.

Luckily, none of his friends were present, which was what he had been hoping for. He was going to try—as Peter had put it—to figure things out.

Last night had been the first in a long time that he had slept in his own bed, and he had missed the feeling of another body next to him. While Clive refused to believe it was his attraction to both men and women that was a problem, he had acknowledged some time during the early hours of that morning that there was *something* that needed fixing.

He ordered his usual red from the bar, and then tucked himself into the corner of the room. He eased into the big leather chair, put his glasses on top of his thick brown hair, and looked down at the scratches on the table, all of them signs of people having sat in that very chair—though he was alone in it now. He was rather well hidden in the armchair under the stairs, but after twenty minutes a pair of heels could be heard clicking towards him. He kept his eyes on the newspaper someone had left on the table, despite being unable to read the words without his glasses, in the hope that whoever it was would see the table was occupied and move on. No such luck.

'Hello again,' said the indirect cause of Clive's gloomy mood.

Clive looked up, and his eyes narrowed slightly. This woman was the last person that he wanted to talk to. He rubbed his eyes, reminding himself that this wasn't *actually* her fault. He cleared his throat, remembering his manners.

'Hello . . . Eleanor?' he tried, his face contorting into an *"Am I right?"* expression.

The woman gasped, bringing a hand up to her heart.

'You wound me, sir. It's Evelyn,' she said, though she was still smiling. 'Where are your friends this evening?'

Evelyn looked around the small pub. Clive suspected it was more for show than anything. He gestured to the seat across from him as he answered.

'It's just me this evening.' He tried to smile, though he doubted it was as successful as he would have liked. He brought his glasses back down on to his nose.

Evelyn placed her glass onto a coaster and sat in the offered seat.

'So what brings you back to this delightful hole in the wall without your friends in tow?' she asked, her eyes sparkling from the reflection of the cheap chandelier hanging above them.

Clive, who hadn't been expecting the question, stalled by taking a sip—or rather a gulp—of his wine and fidgeted in his chair while he deliberated his answer.

'I came here to figure some things out, I guess,' he eventually said, echoing Peter's earlier words.

Evelyn pursed her lips sympathetically.

'Girl problems?' she teased, her facial expressions changing so quickly that Clive thought she must be an actress.

Which, of course, immediately sent his thoughts back to Peter.

'Quite the opposite, actually,' he admitted, his hazel eyes glancing up nervously from under his glasses, gauging her reaction and whether or not she had understood.

Evelyn nodded, comprehension crossing her features.

'I owe myself a drink,' she said quietly, one side of her mouth turning up into a smile.

'Excuse me?' Clive was lost.

'I owe myself a drink. I had a bet with myself that you were a . . .' She waved her hand, searching for the word. '. . . a friend of Dorothy, as you say.'

'How do *you* know that term?' Clive questioned further, genuinely curious.

'She and my brother were practically best friends, darling,' she explained, and Clive smiled sincerely.

'I see,' he chuckled, but it caught in his throat when he picked up on the past tense.

'What happened?' he asked gently.

Evelyn inhaled deeply, her hand flitting to her hair briefly, which was braided across the base of her hairline.

'Michael was caught during a police raid on a club, and was put into prison for a few days.' She picked at one of the paper napkins on the table, ripping it and making a pile with the pieces. 'He was then given the choice between a prison sentence or hormone treatment at Greymore.'

Clive flinched, having heard far too many horror stories about that place both recently and in the past. Evelyn nodded, as though she could read his mind.

'It's a god-awful place, Greymore; Michael hated going there for his injections. Both because of the reason for his visits, but also because the other patients really affected him. He was a compassionate man, so seeing them treated so awfully really played on his mind.'

After a brief pause, Evelyn let out a shaky breath as she continued, 'Then his partner left him when he started growing breasts—because of the hormones—and Michael got depressed. It was painful to see him so . . .' She trailed off, looking to Clive for understanding.

He nodded, one side of his mouth turning up in a sympathetic smile.

'He stopped eating at first.' She smiled sadly, as though the worst had yet to come at that stage. 'Then he started hurting himself.'

Clive gasped. He couldn't help it.

'I found him in his bath, one year and three months ago today.' Evelyn's eyes were unfocused, as though she were back in the memory.

Clive reached out and touched her hand. Her eyes found his again, and she smiled weakly. He gave her fingers a squeeze, deciding to change the subject.

'And what made you think that *I* was . . .' He waved his hand rather than saying it aloud, flipping his short hair dramatically.

Evelyn laughed, grateful for the distraction.

'Well, you gave *me* the cold shoulder, which was my first clue.' At Clive's wince she reassured him, 'oh I was only heartbroken for a second, darling, then I saw you walk back to your table and the hips were my second clue.' She took a sip of her wine, though her eyes showed her glee at teasing her newfound friend.

Clive groaned. 'Is it really that bad?' His friends had pointed this out to him before, but he has assumed they were joking, or exaggerating.

Evelyn allowed a mischievous smile to play at her lips, but didn't answer, instead moving on to her next question.

'So what's wrong in boy town?'

Clive sat across from the young brunette woman, dragging his finger around the rim of his glass.

'He's worried that I'm going to leave him for a woman, just because it's more acceptable.' He sighed, scratching his day-old face hair.

Evelyn shrugged, 'I can understand that,' she admitted evenly.

Clive looked up in confusion. *Isn't she supposed to be on my side? Isn't that one of the rules of making new friends?* His furrowing brow was enough for his companion to feel the need to clarify.

'I mean, if it were me, I'd worry that you would leave me for a man—since that's something I can't compete with as a woman.' She raised her eyebrows, hoping Clive understood her angle.

He shook his head in disagreement. 'But it's not about liking both breasts and chest hair, it's about liking people regardless of those things. He has no reason to feel like he can't compete with a woman just because he's a man.'

Evelyn smiled warmly. 'And have you ever explained it to him like that?' she asked, though she suspected she already knew the answer.

Clive looked baffled for a moment, trying to recall the moment he had, but coming up empty.

'Oh.'

'Yes, "Oh."' She was still smiling, and reached her hand across the table to squeeze his. 'So go tell him, you twit.'

Clive smiled, squeezing her hand. Then his eyes widened as he glanced behind her, and his eyebrows rose in surprise. Evelyn looked over her shoulder, seeing the men from Clive's table yesterday walking through the door. She noticed two—a brown haired man with curly hair, and another with a close trim blonde beard—were standing closer together than the situation warranted, and the third man, who had his red hair slicked back was walking just behind them. She turned back to Clive.

'Is your one the red head?' she asked, winking.

Clive felt his neck go warm, and he tugged at his ear lobe nervously. 'Yeah, that would be him.'

'Michael would have fought you like a rabid dog for that one.' She laughed quietly.

Clive grinned back at her then watched with rapt attention as Peter made his way towards the bar.

Peter was smiling as he ordered his drink, but his smile fell when he scanned the room and saw Clive with the woman they had fought over just last night.

Realising how his current position must look, Clive stood, excusing himself, which Evelyn waved off, and started towards the tall red head.

Peter's jaw clenched as he turned on his heel, heading for the front door after murmuring something to George. He was gone before Clive could cross the room, but he was determined to follow him and clarify. Before he could, his chest was covered by George's muscular forearm.

'Let him go, Clive,' he said quietly.

'But I need to tell him . . . It wasn't what it looked like . . . we were talking about her brother . . . and she told me how to explain things to Peter . . . I wasn't . . .'

George squeezed his bicep, turning his torso slightly so that they were face to face.

'We know, Clive. We believe you.' Tom nodded his agreement. 'But you know what Peter's like. Come over tomorrow, okay?' George's eyes were kind as he spoke. 'We were planning on going to Greymore after a quick stop here, to see if we can visit Tom's friend from school, so we've got to go and catch up with Peter.'

Clive nodded, though his eyes were still locked on the door that Peter had just walked out of.

'Come over tomorrow, Clive, and we'll calm Peter down in the meantime. We'll tell him he has nothing to worry about, and that you'll explain it when you come over,' Tom added, and George smiled over at him.

Clive sighed, knowing they were right. For all his confidence in life, Peter was an insecure man when it came to relationships. Clive realised he should have tried to make him feel safer a long time ago.

'I'll see you tomorrow,' he exhaled, and then turned back to his table under the stairs to retrieve his coat.

George and Tom each patted him on the shoulders as he walked away from them, before turning to leave, themselves.

'That was my fault, wasn't it, darling?' Evelyn's smooth face wrinkled into a frown when Clive returned to the table.

He shook his head softly.

'Not really. Peter is . . .' he searched for the word, 'he's insecure, and also stubborn. My friends are right in getting me to wait until he's calmed down before talking to him.' He smiled at her as he sat back down.

He pressed his fingers into his forehead; tomorrow morning seemed too far away. He looked up at the pretty brunette woman opposite him.

'You know, Evelyn. I'm glad you flirted with me yesterday, talking with you today has been very eye-opening.' He winked, deciding to be happy about the prospect of fixing things with Peter at all.

'Oh, darling, if I had really been flirting, your Peter wouldn't have stood a chance.' She wiggled her perfectly shaped eyebrows before laughing her musical laugh.

Clive was startled awake by someone shaking him. He jolted into consciousness and his body immediately kick-started its "fight" response. He swung his arms wildly—not being the most adept fighter—before the sleepy haze clouding his normally bad eyesight cleared, and he realised it was Tom. He sat up, no longer worried about being attacked, and wiped his eyes.

'Sorry,' his voice was husky, but he managed to sound sheepish as he reached for his glasses on the bedside table.

'It's alright, you missed.' Tom was perched on the side of the bed, his mouth pulled down in a frown. Seeing the look on Tom's face reminded Clive that it wasn't an everyday occurrence having his friend use his emergency key to wake him up.

'What's wrong?' Clive was immediately alert, despite the lack of coffee in his system. He swung his legs out of bed and pulled on the trousers that had lay abandoned on the floor from last night.

'You need to promise that you won't freak out,' Tom said softly, his palms held up and facing Clive in a surrender-like pose.

Clive raised an eyebrow as he pulled on a light blue button up shirt.

'I promise to try,' he admitted, knowing he couldn't make such an agreement without having all the details.

'Close enough,' Tom sighed, 'Peter's in the hospital-'

'What?' Clive shouted, rushing to get his shoes on.

'It looks bad. He got beaten up after we split up to head home last night. We only found him because we had picked up his keys after being searched going into Greymore, and he had forgotten to take them back before he left.' Tom's eyes were tearing up.

Clive was stunned for a moment. Tom wasn't someone who cried. He slipped his arms into a jumper, puling it over his head before he took his friend's hand.

'It is not your fault.' Clive's tone left no room for argument.

Tom nodded sadly. 'Okay,' he exhaled.

Clive finished buttoning up his coat, and then put his hand on the other brunette's shoulder.

'Let's go.'

The hospital was bright. Too bright, considering Peter's life was slowly dimming. Clive opened the hallway door quietly, seeing that George was sat in a chair against the wall, Tom having gone to the end of the hall for a "much needed cigarette".

'How is he?' Clive pulled off his coat and placed it onto the chair next to his friend.

'Looks like internal bleeding last we heard. They're refusing to tell us too much though.' George sighed, pressing his fingertips to his forehead. 'Luckily the matron came by earlier and gave us a summary, but that's all we know.' George looked apologetic, though the lack of information wasn't his fault.

Clive peered through the glass that extended from waist height, almost reaching the top of the dividing wall. He couldn't see Peter; he was curtained off in one of the beds. He tugged at his ear lobe.

Two doctors in their pristine white coats walked by them, clipboards in hand. Both Clive and George were able to overhear the conversation that occurred after the pair scowled in their direction.

'Visiting that queer bloke, I bet,' the skinny, dark haired man muttered.

'A couple of years ago, we could have just carted them off to Greymore,' the blonde added.

The two friends sat in heavy silence, waiting for the doctors to clear the hallway.

'How do you and Tom do it?' Clive asked, considering his friend closely.

'We drink a lot,' George laughed, and Clive chuckled with him.

As their laughter quieted, George's face turned serious.

'We mostly keep to ourselves. We don't seek anyone else's approval. We just accept and support each other. What more *can* you do?' he concluded, and Clive accepted just how amazing his friends were for not letting anyone's judgments separate them.

Clive ran a hand through his hair. George and Tom were his heroes, and he decided in that moment to be more like them. He rolled up his shirtsleeves.

'Well, I'm going to go and apologise to that wonderful man in there for not making him feel more secure.' He gestured to the door leading to the hospital room then moved towards it, briefly placing his hand on George's shoulder, who in turn placed his own on top.

'Good luck. He's a stubborn bastard. Love him, but he's stubborn.'

Clive smiled for a moment before sighing, 'I know.'

He stepped into the hospital room, and George meandered off to try and find Tom. After peeking around several curtains, and profusely apologising to a rather distressed woman, Clive finally found Peter's bed. He brought a chair over from the other side of the room, and sat himself next to Peter's head. His handsome face looked deathly pale, minus the dark purple bruising that had formed around his temple and cheekbone. His eyes were closed, and he looked almost peaceful.

'So, I figured things out, Peter. Finally.' He exhaled a breath, though it wanted to be a laugh. 'Love, I want the thousand extra problems that come with being with you.'

He reached a hand out and brushed the usually slicked-back hair out of his lover's face. He still considered Peter his lover, regardless of their recent argument. A crease formed in Clive's brow. The few machines that had been wheeled in around the bed were flashing, but silent. When George had visited his mother in hospital, he had recalled how much of a racket the few machines had made.

Clive slipped his hand into the one Peter had resting on his chest. His eyes filled with tears, and he had to push his glasses onto his head.

'But I was too late. You did say you wouldn't wait forever.'

Peter's lifeless body couldn't answer him.

1970-80s

AND THE FRIEND CALLED DEREK

CHARLES' HANDS SHOOK as he took the offered leaflet from me. I had known when picking up the small folded paper that my actions would be taken negatively. But the increasingly scrawny man in front of me had moved into my guesthouse almost six months ago, and it was killing me to watch him deteriorate. Ever since Amber died, he had become more withdrawn. He had not returned to work, and resembled a panicked deer whenever unexpected social interaction arose.

Prior to her death, Amber had been the one supporting Charles. His . . . condition was not a result of her passing, but rather it was amplified afterwards. It was only now that I could appreciate how much patience that woman must have had. That's not to say that Charles was completely dependent, it's more that there were a plethora of daily tasks that could set off his anxieties. Talking on the phone was the first one I had really noticed. It had been me that had arranged most of Amber's funeral, simply because even thinking about using the phone made my best friend break out into a cold sweat.

The decision to take a more direct approach had transpired when *E.T. the Extra-Terrestrial* was finally in English cinemas, and despite being the one who had ranted about how good it was supposed to be, Charles talked himself out of going.

Charles ran his free hand through his dirty blond hair, making its natural waviness more prominent.

'I don't need this, Derek. It's only bad right now because-' his words caught in his throat.

'Charlie, it's been seven months. This isn't getting better, and I can only do so much to help. So let me help you to help yourself. Please?' I urged.

Both of our eyes filled up, the stress of the last few months catching up with us now we were acknowledging it.

'But—' he started.

'No buts, Charlie,' I interrupted gently.

I had decided being firm was the best way to get through to him.

'I have silently supported you for seven months, just giving you what you need. And I will continue to do that—you know I will—but you need to help yourself as well, buddy.'

Charlie sighed, but after a long stretch of silence, he eventually nodded slightly.

'I didn't mean to make you my new wife, Derek.' He breathed a laugh, sniffing loudly.

I chuckled.

'It's alright, I happen to be a rather brilliant wife.'

He laughed a little louder, before his eyes unfocused and he remained quiet for a few moments.

I mentally cursed myself for the slip up, despite the fact that he had initiated the joke.

'I'm sorry . . .' I began, but he looked up at me as though he hadn't realised that he'd taken a momentary step away from reality.

'No,' he spoke softly, and one corner of his mouth turned up in a smile, 'you *are* a rather brilliant wife.'

We smiled at each other tenatively, and I wiped at my eyes slightly, removing any evidence of tears.

'I'll call for an appointment tomorrow?' he asked, because even though he had used the first person, we both knew I'd still be the one making the call.

'Tomorrow morning,' I agreed. 'I'm sure Greymore will do you the world of good.'

'My friend Derek,' he murmured, wiping his hooked nose with the cuff of his grey woven blazer, 'you're too good to me.'

I placed my hand on his bicep and squeezed firmly, exhaling heavily as relief rushed through me.

AND THE TWO SIDES OF A COIN

Monday 9:00am
SESSION 1

DOCTOR APRIL HAWKE sat behind her desk, exasperated. Every Monday she'd find new patient profiles scattered across the table, and she'd bet a month's wages that Baxter did it on purpose; ignoring the "in" tray she had for such things. She shuffled around in her cold plastic chair, irritated as her bum started going numb after a few moments. Despite being a career minded woman—to the point that she'd put off having children until her thirties and had dedicated her life to becoming a Doctor of Mental Health—she still had a crappy seat. Even Jason the Intern's chair was cushioned. *Sexist bastards,* she thought before moving to organise her desk.

At exactly 9:15am there was a series of timid knocks on Doctor Hawke's open door. She looked up to see a shy looking young woman standing in the doorway, shifting her weight uncomfortably. Doctor Hawke stood and beckoned the new patient into the office. The young woman cleared her throat, her eyes darting to the still-open door. April understood the hint and moved around the patient to close it.

'Good morning,' she greeted, holding out her hand for the woman to shake. 'I'm Doctor Hawke.'

The two women, age difference aside, looked very similar. Both had a curvaceous figure, though Doctor Hawke wore a fitted blouse and pencil skirt to accentuate this whereas the patient wore an unflattering, oversized jumper and an un-shapely skirt that fell to her calves.

'Hello. I . . . I don't shake hands,' the woman stammered, looking anywhere but at the outstretched fingers and clutching her handbag as though it were a lifeline.

Doctor Hawke's smile barely faltered, and she motioned to the seat opposite her own. Mrs. Jenkins—the doctor noted her name as she glanced at her appointment book— sat in the chair dutifully and folded her hands on her lap.

Hawke wasn't blind to the fact that she always got the majority of female referrals. She found it ironic that men assume they have a monopoly on all knowledge, as though they were made in the image of the male God's omniscience; while women are frivolous, feeble followers. Yet men's ineptitude turns them into frightened little boys when faced with the female psyche.

'How are you?' the doctor asked politely; she wasn't going to let her chauvinistic colleagues affect her professionalism or empathy.

'I'm fine, thank you,' the patient replied submissively.

'Mrs. Jenkins, would you mind telling me why you were referred to Greymore?'

'Don't you have that information already?'

'Yes,' the Doctor smiled patiently, 'but I'd like you to tell me as well.'

The young woman's porcelain cheeks flushed, and she brought her hands—red raw from excoriation—to her face in an attempt to cool them down. As she realised they were visible, she tentatively hid them behind her handbag.

'My husband finds some of the things I do to be a waste of time,' Mrs. Jenkins offered, clearly not prepared to go into details without being asked.

'What sort of things?' Dr. Hawke invited.

'For instance, I have to wash my hands ten times a day at regular intervals, and I check the lock on the front door every time I go in or out of the house,' she disclosed, momentarily forgetting her hands to push a rebellious wisp of hair behind her ear.

'How many times do you check the lock?'

'Five times.'

Doctor Hawke was scratching down notes as the conversation developed. She found herself writing mostly numbers; "washes hands ten times a day", "checks lock on the door five times", "only gets out of bed when the minutes past the hour are a multiple of ten". As the new patient recalled details of her regimented life, the Doctor realised she would have to find a way through the numbers and into Mrs Jenkins' mind-set. A relationship of trust would need to be built so that Mrs Jenkins may confide her fears and the underlying story of why the compulsions began. Hawke believed a rapport between Doctor and patient was a vital factor for improvement of symptoms and mental state.

'It's important that you have a support network—' Doctor Hawke started.

'My husband actually recommended I come and see you, to try and . . .' she paused, 'to try and get help for my problems.'

The words seemed rehearsed, but Doctor Hawke smiled warmly all the same, trying to ease her new patient. Despite her healthy weight, she looked so frail, holding herself in a way that made her similar to a timid child. *The obsessive compulsions have clearly knocked her confidence,* the doctor thought, observing Mrs Jenkins' inward posture.

'I think the best course of action is to meet with you once a fortnight initially to try some behavioural therapy. Specifically something called exposure and response prevention. Is this time good for you, or would you prefer a different time?'

'This time is fine, thank you.' Her response was hesitant, but she smiled politely.

'Excellent; here's my card in case you need to cancel or re-arrange appointments, or if you have any general questions. It has my work number extension line which you can reach me on from nine until five.' Doctor Hawke handed a small white card across the desk. 'And this is a leaflet on the type of therapy we're going to be doing,' she continued.

Mrs Jenkins hesitantly accepted them, being careful to ensure their hands didn't come into contact.

'Thank you, Doctor.' The young woman offered a strained smile and dropped the card and leaflet into her bag; her hands shaking and failing to disguise the nauseated expression that passed over her features. 'Could you please direct me to the ladies bathroom?' she asked; her face paling and the desperation in her voice clear.

'Certainly. From here if you take the second left it's the first door around that corner.'

11:45am
RUTH JENKINS

Ruth took a handkerchief out of her bag and used it as a barrier between her hand and the doorknob. She wiped each foot on the doormat five times before shutting the door behind her. Lock, unlock, lock, unlock, lock, unlock, lock, unlock, lock. The light switch next to the door made a soothing click as she flicked it on and off ten times before moving to the next light switch. Flittering around the house, she checked the frame of the windows, applying pressure to ensure they couldn't be pried open. Ruth's mind drifted to the doctor's words . . . *It's important that you have a support network* . . . She thought about how happy Steven had been when she'd told him she'd booked an appointment at Greymore. As her mind returned to her current task she scolded herself for losing count of how many times she'd checked the window. Sighing, she started again; one, two, three, four, five.

Only having to restart the checks once more, Ruth padded into the small bathroom just an hour later, glared at the horrid yellow tiles and removed her clothes. After carefully folding each item and placing the pile on the toilet seat, she turned the shower to its hottest setting, climbed into the bathtub and hesitantly stepped under the spray. Ruth hissed as the water pelted her pale skin. The heat was unbearable and caused her raw flesh to sting. Continuing the self-inflicted torture, she reached for the wash-brush, applied soap and began vigorously scrubbing herself. The sharp bristles scratched, biting away at her sore flesh. Barely healed, the stretched skin of her scars began to weep. Ruth sobbed—the water washing away her whimpers.

5:30pm
APRIL HAWKE

April rolled her shoulders, attempting to ease the tension she had been carrying there. Hearing the satisfactory click of her bones, she rolled her neck from side to side. Another click. Turning her key in the front door, she huffed angrily as she thought back to her day.

"You get the majority of women clients to cover our asses. If they see a woman doctor, they can't complain we're brushing them and their symptoms aside based on their gender. It makes you a great asset to this place, Hawke." Bob sat in his big comfy chair, arms attempting to cross over his seemingly ever-growing belly. A still-lit cigarette sat in an ashtray, already filled to the brim with ash and butts. April glared at Bob as he tried to brush her complaint aside, ironically as he'd just described, because she was a woman.

April rolled her shoulders again as she stepped into the house and slipped off her heels. She cracked her knuckles before putting the kids' discarded shoes onto their mats. She grumbled, reminding herself of the countless times she had told Clarissa about the shoe mats. April conjured a smile as she heard small footsteps scampering across the upstairs hallway and down the stairs. Two grinning children tackled her, and she quickly moved to ensure they weren't hurt.

'Be careful you two,' she said gently, looking pointedly at her son. He dropped his eyes to the floor, avoiding his mother's gaze.

'Mom,' Jessica drew out in a whiney voice, 'you don't let us do anything since James got sick—but he's better now.' She looked to her older brother and smiled up at him. 'Stop being worried!'

The small girl patted her mother's leg softly before running back upstairs. James gave his mother a queasy smile before following her, though deliberately walking carefully instead of running.

'That girl's wise beyond her years.'

April jumped as the nanny's Irish accent broke the silence. The doctor stared at the young woman, startled that she'd be so outright.

'You should get yourself home before it becomes much darker, Ms McKay,' she uttered bluntly.

Clarissa swallowed hard as she realised she had overstepped and immediately felt bad.

'I'm sorry Mrs Hawke, I didn't mean—' she stumbled over her words.

April sighed heavily.

'It's quite alright, Clarissa.' She waved a hand dismissively, and the nanny knew she was forgiven by the use of her first name. 'Now I was serious about you getting home. See you in the morning at normal time?'

'Of course!' Clarissa smiled, relieved.

11:00pm
APRIL HAWKE

April flicked the bedroom light off and absently scanned the room as she pulled the duvet back on the bed. Noticing one of the drawers cracked open with a sock poking out of the top, she moved across to the dresser.

'What are you doing, love?' Roy, her husband, asked softly from the doorway.

April jumped.

'Just pushing the draw in properly; the sock would have bugged me all night otherwise.' She motioned to the white sock in her hand, too big to belong to anyone other than the man in the doorway.

Roy laughed, bemused, and climbed into bed. April finished re-arranging the contents of the draw so they lay flat before joining him.

Monday 9:15am
SESSION 2

April looked up as she heard light footsteps approach her office. In a building—hell, an industry—dominated by males, she had been quick to learn how to differentiate between the footsteps of her mostly female clientele and those of her co-workers. Mrs. Jenkins stood awkwardly in the doorway, unable to knock the open door to make her presence known now that eye contact had been made.

'Good morning Ruth, can I call you Ruth?' Doctor Hawke greeted warmly.

The young woman nodded and took a few steps into the small, inadequate office. April was convinced it had once been a supplies cupboard.

'I'd like you to shut the door for me, but only shut it once,' the doctor instructed, getting straight down to business.

Ruth swallowed heavily, her heart pounding in her chest so hard she thought it might burst out. Thinking of the mess it would make, she inhaled slowly, counting to five.

'What will happen if you don't check the door five times?' April continued.

'I don't know,' Ruth sighed, tears threatening to fall and hating the burning sensation at the front of her head that comes with trying to hold them back.

Seeing the young woman's distress, April closed the door gently and motioned for her patient to take a seat in the chair across from hers, which she did. Ruth softly drummed her knuckles on the wooden arm of the chair five times, almost succeeding in going unnoticed.

'Why did you do that?' Doctor Hawke asked, accusation free from her tone.

'Why did I do what?' The patient furrowed her brow, confused.

'The knocking,' April replied simply.

'I didn't knock—the door was already open.' The crease in Ruth's brow deepened.

'I meant on the chair.'

'Oh . . .' Ruth faltered, glancing at her hand and the arm of the chair curiously. 'I guess I was making up for not being able to knock on the door,' she offered lamely, but Doctor Hawke made a note of the action and Mrs Jenkins' explanation nonetheless.

April maintained eye contact with her patient as she reached into her top draw and took out a clean pen. She nonchalantly bit the end of the pen, as if she were pondering something of great importance. Then she set it on the desk next to a pad of paper in front of the young woman.

'Ruth, I would like for you to write as many lines as you can with this pen.'

The young woman paled almost immediately.

'I promise you, I am the only person who has touched it, and I haven't used it prior to taking it out of my draw just now,' April attempted to reassure her. 'Do you think you could at least try?' she urged.

Ruth hesitantly reached for the pen, her skin crawling as her shaking fingers touched the cool plastic, and when her hand brushed against the paper it was as though she could feel her hands becoming dirty. She went to begin but then looked up at the doctor. 'I can't, I'm sorry.' She dropped the pen back onto the desk

'That's alright, that was actually better than I expected.' April smiled. 'You can go and wash your hands now, then we can move on to the next step,' she continued, 'but I want you back in no more than five minutes, do you think that's fair?'

Ruth smiled shyly and nodded, resembling a small child once again before walking out of the office at a reasonable pace to the toilets.

6:00pm
APRIL HAWKE

April rolled her shoulders; the traffic on the way home had made her extra tense. Hearing the satisfactory click of her bones, she rolled her neck from side to side. Another click. Turning her key in the front door, her eyes immediately darted to the shoe mats. *Why do children do the exact opposite of what you tell them?* she thought as she slipped off her heels before placing her daughter's shoes onto the mat, followed by her son's. April shrugged off her coat and placed it on the second hook her husband had nailed to the wall earlier that year. For the first time she noticed the first hook was slightly higher up than the others. Making a note to tell Roy so he could fix it, she moved around the rest of the house. The big rug in the living room—an anniversary present from Roy's parents—was folded at the corner closest to April, so she kicked it back into place as she walked past.

'Clarissa?' she called out, hoping to locate the nanny by the sound of a response.

'Mrs. Hawke?' The reply came from the kitchen, so April followed the sound of the voice, and found the nanny elbow deep in soapy water.

'I'm sorry for getting back a little later than usual, the traffic was horrendous,' the doctor immediately apologised, feeling guilty for making the poor woman stay longer than usual.

Clarissa only smiled and shrugged.

'It was no problem, I assumed you got caught up at work or something so I made the kids some dinner and then I didn't want to leave a mess so I started tidying up-' the Irish woman paused for breath. 'I'm rambling, let me start again. It was no problem.' Clarissa smiled, blowing a few loose strands of hair out of her face.

'Thank you, you've really gone above and beyond this evening.' April smiled, grateful.

Yet she couldn't draw her eyes away from the plates on the drying rack that hadn't been rinsed of soapsuds.

'Anyway, if it's okay, can I get on home now?' Clarissa asked, oblivious to her employer's discomfort.

April nodded and mumbled a dismissal.

'Alright then.' Clarissa drained the sink and dried her hands on a cloth. 'I'll see you tomorrow Mrs. Hawke,' the nanny called over her shoulder as she walked out the kitchen.

April quickly moved over to the sink and turned on the hot tap, rinsing the soapy plates. Once she had dried them and put them back in the cupboard, she wiped down the counter and browsed through the cupboards, curious as to what Clarissa had given the children for dinner. Finally, the last cupboard had a tin of beans missing. Beans on toast then. April took a moment to turn the few tins that had been disturbed back around so their labels were visible.

Happening to glance at the clock hanging above the doorway, she realised it was close to 6:30pm, and Roy still wasn't home. Disregarding any logical reasons for his absence, her mind immediately went to the worst-case scenario. *What if he got into an accident on the way home and no one has found him yet? What if he was overtired and drove his car into a tree and his body was so mangled they haven't been able to identify him yet? What if he had a heart attack at work and Clarissa had missed the phone call because she was making dinner?*

April started biting the already short fingernails of her left hand. Ignoring the taste of blood in her mouth, she continued to rip away at them, despite the ratio of nail to fingertip decreasing dramatically. By the time she heard her husband's greeting from the living room, her left hand was a bloody mess and stung like a bitch.

'Sorry I'm late love,' Roy started as he found her in the kitchen. 'I hope you weren't too worried.' Then his eyes fell to her hand. 'Ah crap, April, not again. Let's get that bandaged up.'

8:00pm
RUTH JENKINS

The room was a blur as Steven spun her around in his arms. Ruth had told him about her slowly progressing therapy with Doctor Hawke over dinner, and he'd been so proud when she told him about picking up the pen that he'd come over and picked her up, spinning her around their living room. Ruth couldn't help but laugh as she went dizzy, her husband's pride apparently rubbing off. What shocked her more than her compliance with being picked up was that she was able to return to her dinner and finish the meal before the need to wash her hands became overwhelming. *Apparently a strong support network really does help,* she thought.

Monday 9:30am
SESSION 12

April sat behind her desk and tried not to gawp at the young woman who had been so shy and vulnerable when she first walked into her office. Now, it was fair to say that Ruth Jenkins had started to become a much more confidant person. She had been able to knock the door and close it behind her when she arrived, and had told the doctor of her ability to go for longer durations before washing her hands and only having to do her checks once. It was glaringly obvious that Doctor Hawke was impressed, which only seemed to make Ruth glow more so.

This remarkable turnaround inspired April to jump ahead a few stages in the exposure/response treatment. She took out a handkerchief and pushed it across the desk towards the young woman. When unfolded, it revealed a deep red stain.

'I've put blood on it; we have butcher shops send us it for cases such as yours. It's clear of disease, so there's no way it can cause you any harm.' Doctor Hawke explained softly.

The change in Ruth's composure was astonishing. She'd gone from starting to appear comfortable in her own skin to being more withdrawn than when she had first been referred to Greymore. April immediately regretted her actions, but for fear of seeming unprofessional she decided to continue—cautiously.

'I'd like you to hold this for as long as possible,' she began, motioning to the handkerchief. 'Then if it becomes too much, I'd like for you to stay here as long as you feel you can between putting it down and going to wash your hands, okay?'

Ruth swallowed the bile that had risen to her throat and nodded slowly. Before even moving to pick up the hankie her body began to shake violently. Her hand trembled as it touched the silk material and tears flooded her eyes as she thought about the thousands of germs now on her skin. She felt contaminated; the knowledge that the skin on her hands was permanently raw and cracked made her increasingly nauseous. Her heart hammered in her ribcage. The image of the blood seeping through her wounded hand and into her own bloodstream was more than Ruth could handle. She was embarrassed as she realised she'd broken into a noticeable sweat.

She tossed the handkerchief back onto the desk, indifferent about where or how it landed and fled to the women's bathroom. She spent some time throwing up the contents of her stomach into one of the cubicle toilets before moving across to the sinks.

Ruth washed her hands first—thankful for the boiling hot water, and then splashed soapy water onto the hot tap before cleansing her hands a second time. She then proceeded to wash her hands a further eight times, demonstrating how much the task had distressed her.

When she staggered back into Doctor Hawke's office nearly half an hour later, her face looked pasty and hair clung to her damp forehead. April was guilt-ridden. It was too soon. Mortified with herself, she organised a taxi for Mrs. Jenkins and paid the fare personally.

Once Ruth had gratefully slipped into the taxi, Doctor Hawke returned to her office. She closed the door behind her and leant against it for a minute. Pushing her hair behind her ears, she moved to the bookshelves behind her desk and scanned over them quickly as if they'd somehow un-alphabetised themselves in the ten minutes she'd been out of the room.

6:30pm
APRIL HAWKE

April shrugged her coat off and hung it up on the second coat hook before slipping off her shoes, placing them on the mat. She called out her apologies for being late, but was met with no response. Frowning, she took the stairs two at a time and checked Jessie and James' rooms. Nothing. She poked her head into her own room, for once wishing they'd broken the rule of "no playing in mom and dad's room". No sign of them in there either though. Running back down the stairs and slipping on the last one, she searched the living room and kitchen after regaining her footing. The house was empty. Panicking, she ran back into the hallway, threw on her coat and shoved her feet into some trainers. Her urgency meant the sides folded inwards uncomfortably. As she spun to open the front door after only entering it five minutes earlier, her eyes focused on the note.

> *April, taken James to the hospital.*
> *Will explain later and call when I know something.*
> *Don't worry, Roy x*

Despite her husband's assurances, the adrenaline from dashing around the house and the newly evoked fear for her son caused April's breath to come in short gasps. When the threat of hyperventilating almost became a reality, she forced herself to count as she inhaled.

1, 2, 3, 4, 5.

She exhaled. She repeated this until the oxygen debt had been repaid. The doctor took her coat and shoes off for the second time that evening and began pacing around the hallway, waiting for the Roy's call.

Half an hour later, the shrill ringing of the phone made April freeze mid-step. The realisation that she'd not stopped pacing indicated she hadn't been able to calm herself down as much as she had thought. When the phone rang out, she cursed softly.

Answering the damn thing usually helps . . . Luckily, it rang a second time and she snatched it up within seconds.

'Hello?' she rasped.

'Hi sweetheart.' Her husband's voice sounded strained. 'James needs to stay overnight for some tests. The doctor thinks it might be a relapse. Could you bring an overnight bag for him?' His question fell on deaf ears.

April's hand flew to her chest, the phone falling from her hand. She collapsed in a heap; hyperventilating was again becoming a serious possibility. She was still able to hear Roy calling out her name, despite the phone now lying slightly out of reach. Shakily, she crawled across the carpet and tentatively placed it against her ear.

'April? Are you still there, love?'

April flinched as she realised how unhelpful she was being.

'Yes, sorry. I just–'

'I know. But we have to pull ourselves together. For James, okay?'

April could tell Roy was trying to sound strong; she pictured him having to look on as their son was hooked up to various machines and tubes. She inhaled slowly.

'Right. Overnight bag. Where's Jessie?' April asked as an afterthought, uncomfortable with the idea of Jessie having to be at the hospital.

'I dropped her off at my parents' house. They've said they will have her until tomorrow,' Roy explained easily.

'Okay. I'll be over as soon as possible.'

The call disconnected. April squared her shoulders and walked up the stairs with what she hoped was a composed demeanor. She stepped into James' room and the calm facade shattered. She scrambled through his drawers, unable to think of what he would need. *Would he want his blue t-shirt or the green? What if I pack the blue and he dies? The green then.* April's eyes began to water and a headache quickly developed as a result of fighting the tears back. Her brain was playing out every possible scenario in her head and sobs began to rock her body. She fell to her knees heavily, the searing pain that shot up her legs going unnoticed. She shuffled around on the floor until her knees were brought up to her chin and she hugged them tightly. The overnight bag forgotten, April rocked slightly in her son's room, already imagining life without him.

9:30pm
RUTH JENKINS

Ruth kept her eyes to the floor as she recalled her morning at Greymore to Steven. When she finally brought herself to look up at him, his face had gone a deep shade of red, eerily similar to the colour of the blood on the handkerchief that still haunted her.

'But you'd been doing so well,' her husband spluttered.

Ruth's eyes fell back to the floor as she shrugged, hoping his disappointment wouldn't last.

After a series of heavy sighs, he continued. 'Let's just go to bed, yeah?'

Ruth nodded, and moved towards the front door to start her checks as always before going to bed. This, however, only sparked anger in her husband.

'No, no bloody checks. The world isn't going to end if you don't do your sodding checks!'

Ruth was startled. Steven had never gotten angry with her, and the spittle in the corners of his lips was distracting.

'But I have to, Steven. I'll only be five minutes, you go-' she tried to defend herself, but he'd already thrown his hands up in the air desperately and left.

Ruth's eyes filled with tears as she moved towards the front door, subconsciously pushing her hair behind her ear. Through blurred vision she started her checks, but Steven's outburst echoed in her mind causing her to lose count. Unable to bite back the tears she let them fall, and in a burst of frustration she slammed her fists off the wall before turning and sliding to the floor. She sobbed, her body shaking and her hands covering her mouth as if to silence herself. Ruth replayed her conversation with Steven in her head dozens of times, hating herself for being so pathetic and causing his disappointment. Her mother had always told her that she was weak. That she'd never be able to make Steven happy. Ruth couldn't even stand up to finish her checks—let alone allow Steven to do much more than sleep beside her. She sniffed, weeping harder as she realised the truth of her mother's words.

2:00am

She had been sat on the floor staring blankly for hours. Deciding how to do it. Wiping the still wet tears from her face, she pulled herself up to her feet. She slowly walked into the kitchen, swiped the car keys on the side and swung open the door that led into the garage, closing it as quietly as possible behind her. Her movements were calculated and calm as she mechanically plucked the duct tape from its position on a shelf. The hose was mounted to the wall awkwardly, but after a moment of struggle she managed to tug it down. It didn't take long for her to secure the hose to the exhaust pipe of the car, a little extra time taken to make sure there were no gaps in the tape. She then opened the driver's side door and cracked the window, sliding the other end of the hose through it, using a few strips of tape to keep it in place and block the gaps as best as she could. Sliding into the driver's seat, she closed the door and turned on the engine.

There would be no mess and no note.

For the first time in a long time, she felt calm, at peace even. All the anxieties seemed insignificant now. Finally she felt in control of her own life. A yawn escaped her lips, and she settled herself into the chair, prepared to finally go to sleep. Her eyes fluttered closed, and she wrapped her arms around herself to fight off the chill.

She sighed—content—and drifted.

ACKNOWLEDGMENTS

SINCE THIS IS my first publication, I'm going to go wild and thank everyone, so if you read all of this, you deserve an overpriced coffee. Or tea, whichever you prefer.

I would first and foremost like to thank Gemma, who has read countless drafts, random trains of thought, and my panicked ramblings regarding this book. She's definitely my writing Yoda.

I'd like to thank Naomi, for taking my author's photo at stupid-o'clock in the morning, and also for putting up with me when we're about to watch a film, but I then pause it without warning and start scribbling over whatever is closest. Her patience is almost unlimited. Almost.

Arathi and Caitlin, you guys were my test audience, so thank you for being gentle in all the right places. Also, Becki, Ellie, Holly, James, Mason, Matt, Mpho, Paige, Robyn and Roxy, for suffering through the trials and tribulations of being my friends. I imagine it's as hard for you as it is for me.

Amanda and Tom, my college teachers, for giving me support and pointers during the original writing of this book. Also thank you Julia, for smiling every single day.

Thank you to all the people who allowed me to interview you during my research—you know who you are. Without your knowledge this book wouldn't exist.

My family are pretty decent as well, so thanks you guys. You've got some rather good genes and I am grateful to have received them.

My sister, Kate—because we make dance routines to my iTunes playlist, you steal my clothes, and you are unfortunate enough to look like me. I know you're thinking, "Except I'm prettier."

My brother, Ross, you get a mention because a) you've survived a house full of females, and for that I commend you and b) because if I only included Kate, Mom would shout at me and you'd use it as leverage.

18193027R00060

Printed in Great Britain
by Amazon